UNCLE SHAWN AND BILL

UNCLE SHAWN AND BILL

AND THE PAJIMMINY-CRIMMINY UNUSUAL ADVENTURE

← SHY BADGER DANCING

A. L. KENNEDY

ILLUSTRATED BY GEMMA CORRELL

Kane Miller
A DIVISION OF EDC PUBLISHING

First American Edition 2018
Kane Miller, A Division of EDC Publishing

Text © 2018 A. L. Kennedy
Illustrations © 2018 Gemma Correll
Published by arrangement with Walker Books Limited, London.

For information contact:
Kane Miller, A Division of EDC Publishing
P.O. Box 470663
Tulsa, OK 74147-0663
www.kanemiller.com
www.edcpub.com
www.usbornebooksandmore.com

Library of Congress Control Number: 2017958227

Printed and bound in the United States of America
1 2 3 4 5 6 7 8 9 10
ISBN: 978-1-61067-741-7

For VDB

BLUEBERRY-
FLAVORED
← BURP

SECTION ONE

*In which everyone on Uncle Shawn's llama farm,
way up on the sunny side of Scotland, is so happy
their toes feel ticklish. It really couldn't be a better
day for everyone. We wouldn't expect a dangerous
and terrible adventure to start happening all over
the place on a day as nice as this. Or would we…?*

Brian Llama had just eaten six pints of blueberry jam and was lying in the warm grass of his
meadow feeling a bit full. He was just burping a
blueberry-flavored burp when he heard a slippery
kind of voice saying, "We can't have that. Llamas
in Scotland. That's definitely Unusual."

7

SUSPICIOUS STRANGER

CONCERNED RABBIT

UNEASY WEASEL

SCARED SPIDER

Brian raised his head and saw a stranger peering over the hedge. The stranger was wearing a perfectly white suit and perfectly shiny black shoes and had perfectly polished fingernails that glittered in the sun as he wrote something down with a silvery pencil into a tiny, clean notebook.

The strange man stared at Brian as if he was some kind of horrible mistake, like a trampoline covered in squirrels. He spoke again and wrote down another note. "And a llama with bright-blue

8

BRAVE LLAMA

WORRIED SISKINS

nose fur. Unusual. Perhaps the beast has a terrible disease. Everyone knows Unusualness leads to terrible disease."

Now Brian was a very brave llama. He had to be, because he was very scared most of the time. Tall shadows and Tuesdays and long sums and swamp monsters ... lots of things scared Brian Llama. And having a terrible disease! That sounded really frightening. And having blue nose fur – that must be the worst disease ever!

"Oh no," thought Brian. "What will I do?" And his fur puffed out with fright so that he looked like a chocolate-colored cloud with hooves and big, scared llama eyes.

The stranger smiled a smile that was as white as a polar bear bottom and almost too wide for his head.

POLAR BEAR (WHITE)

POLAR BEAR BOTTOM (VERY WHITE)

This made Brian run away shouting, "*Waaaaah! EMERGENCIA!*" Which is Spanish for "*Waaaaah! EMERGENCY!*"

Only then he remembered that his nose fur was blue because it was covered with blueberry jam and so he probably wasn't ill. He just had delicious jam to lick off his nose – and whiskers and chin – as far as his clever llama tongue could reach. (One of the best things about being a llama is how much jam you can have left on your nose to eat later.) The jam tasted so wonderful that Brian forgot about the shiny stranger.

Later, Carlos Llama was playing snap with Guinevere Llama and drinking lemonade. They didn't even notice the shiny stranger peeking at them through the hedge. The stranger scratched his ears and his teeth glimmered while he made notes.

And later than that, Ginalolobrigida Llama was arranging her new selection of mascaras in her llama barn. Knowing that she had more mascara than any other llama on earth always made Ginalolobrigida especially happy. She was putting so much effort into looking dainty and lovely that she didn't notice the shiny stranger climbing a tree to stare at her and make even more notes

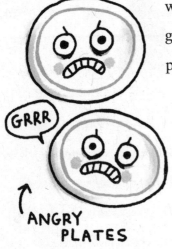

GRRR

ANGRY
PLATES

while his big white teeth gleamed the way angry plates would.

The stranger had a handkerchief over his head.

In case there were spiders. 🐾

SECTION TWO

In which – well – maybe not everyone on the farm is feeling very happy after all. And where on earth is Uncle Shawn? He's really good at rescuing people and adventures. Maybe we'll need him soon.

Badger Bill wanted to play with Uncle Shawn, who was his best friend in the whole wide world. Uncle Shawn was friendly and funny and kind, with his flappy clothes and his floppy arms and his wibbly hair. And he had large, blue, clever eyes that could stare straight through you and find out just what you were like. His eyes were also good at winking.

13

Uncle Shawn's pockets were full of sandy, fluffy toffee that tasted of honey and Saturday afternoons. And Uncle Shawn told Bill jokes like "What happens if you sleep on a corduroy pillow?"

Bill knew the answer to that one: "You make headlines!"

Bill told Uncle Shawn jokes like "What isn't red and doesn't make a noise?"

"NO TOMATOES!" Uncle Shawn always knew the answers to jokes.

If Uncle Shawn and Bill were by the sea that whispered and tickled along the bay below the farm, they would just snuggle their bare feet in the warm sand, or paddle in the shallows, and Uncle Shawn would put shells (and sand) into his pockets (and onto his toffees). The two friends didn't swim, because Bill hadn't learned how yet. Uncle Shawn was going to teach him, because Bill sometimes wanted to be a pirate

CAPTAIN BARTHOLOMEW BADGER

TOILET-
BRUSH
CUTLASS

SPONGE
SAILS

SOAP
BOAT

BATH
PLUG
ANCHOR

and sail the nineteen seas, as counted carefully by Captain Bartholomew Badger. (Captain Bartholomew was the first badger to carve a sailing ship out of soap. It sank as soon as he launched it, but when he had swum back to land, everyone agreed that he looked much cleaner.) Bill thought pirates should probably know how to swim.

But earlier today when Bill had seen Uncle Shawn by the llama barns and asked him to play, Uncle Shawn shook his head and called, "I can't play now, Bill. I'm very busy." While he said this, he was hopping on one big mahogany shoe – plack, plack, plack – and sprinkling sugar on the paths and making clicking noises with his tongue against his teeth. He sounded like someone knitting far away. This seemed an Unusual thing to do.

Later, Bill had seen Uncle Shawn in Fingle Wood. Uncle Shawn was hanging upside down from a tree branch by his knees and counting, "One, two, three, four. One, two, three, four." When Bill came near, Uncle Shawn shook his head and called, "I can't play now, Bill. I'm very busy." This also seemed Unusual to Bill.

16

Then Bill had seen Uncle Shawn by the seashore, up to his trouser knees in the water. He was staring at the waves and patting them. While he did this he let out long noises that sounded a bit like, "*BooWOOoooAAAhh-WahWupWup. BoioioioioioioioiWoahOOP.*" Then Uncle Shawn shook his head and called, "I can't play now, Bill. I'm very busy."

This made Bill feel a bit sad. He thought to himself, "Unusual hopping… Unusual swinging from trees… Unusual patting of waves… That's all… Unusual."

He wriggled his whiskers and thought, "I wonder if Uncle Shawn is Too Unusual?" And then Badger Bill adjusted his small pirate hat, which he was wearing because he wanted to feel like a small pirate.

While these thoughts passed the whole way through Bill's head, through the part of the brain that likes toasted cheese and the part that likes tickles and the Area of Sneezes and onward, the shiny stranger was watching him from under a small bush.

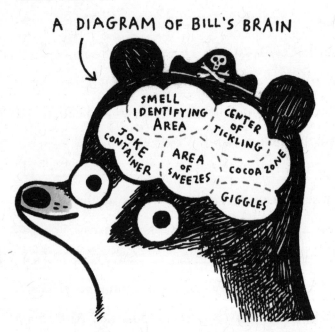

A DIAGRAM OF BILL'S BRAIN

The stranger took out his notebook and wrote: *Small badger. Looks as if he is wearing pirate hat. Completely Unusual!!!* 🐾

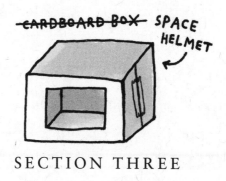

CARDBOARD BOX SPACE HELMET

SECTION THREE

In which we find out more about the shiny

stranger – which is a bit frightening. In fact,

I have a very bad feeling about this man and

his perfectly clean clothes and his glistening teeth.

Later that day, the stranger was walking towards the village of Pandrumdroochit, a few miles north of the llama farm. He was hitting the hedges and bushes with a branch he had found so that he could scare away any animals and birds. He didn't like animals and birds.

The stranger had silky hair that lay very flat on his head, almost as if it were paint and not

SILKY HAIR

GLITTERY DARK-PURPLE EYES (FOR STARING AT UNUSUALNESS)

EARS (LISTENING FOR UNUSUALNESS)

FRIGHTENING SMILE

CRIMSON VEST

SPOTLESS JACKET

FINGER (FOR POINTING AT UNUSUAL PEOPLE HAVING FUN)

EVIL SOCKS

THE SHINIEST SHOES YOU HAVE EVER SEEN

hair at all, and he had glittery dark-purple eyes and a crimson vest, a spotless white jacket and spotless white trousers. His shoes were so shiny it would hurt you to look at them (which is why he kept them like that). While he walked, he smiled a smile that was the size of a polished bathroom sink.

When he saw a small boy called Hughie bouncy-space-walking about with a cardboard box on his head, the stranger's teeth seemed to get even bigger, and you could hear a sort of *skreeee skreeee* noise as they ground against each other.

"What are you doing, horrible boy?" said the stranger.

Hughie looked up at the man through the hole he had cut in the front of the box. "I am a spaceman. I am on the planet Floop and I am

SPACE WALK

21

wearing my space helmet." Hughie was surprised that the man couldn't have worked this out for himself.

The stranger made a note in his book. "The last horrible small boy I met who thought he was a spaceman is now a patient in my Institution for Maximum Security and Unusualness Curing."

"Oh, that wouldn't suit me," said Hughie. "I'm a very busy spaceman and Mum says I never have any patients."

"She means patience," said the stranger.

"Yes. Patients," said Hughie. And he began to bouncy-space-walk up the road as fast as he could, waving his arms to keep away space goblins. 🐾

UNUSUAL-SMELLING DOG

SECTION FOUR

In which we find out what the squeaky-clean stranger who doesn't like anything has been doing in Pandrumdroochit. And what he has been building, hidden away behind the hills. I really hope that Uncle Shawn will be here soon. We'll feel less worried then. I wonder where he is?

The shiny stranger was now in Pandrumdroochit village. As he had done every morning since he arrived, he walked along the main street with neat steps, handing out leaflets. Today's leaflets said:

23

UNUSUALNESS!!!

ARE YOU TROUBLED BY *Unusualness?*

DOES YOUR ICE CREAM TASTE *Unusual?*

DOES YOUR DOG SMELL *Unusual?*

DOES YOUR WHISTLING SOUND *Unusual?*

DO YOU HAVE FRIENDS OR FAMILY WHO SEEM TO BE ... *Unusual?*

Being Unusual is catching AND VERY DANGEROUS.

STOP WHISTLING AT ONCE.

DO <u>NOT</u> TOUCH THE UNUSUAL PERSON, OR ANIMAL, OR ICE CREAM.

Send him, or her, or it directly to the

WORLD-FAMOUS UNUSUALNESS SPECIALIST DR. P'KLAWZ

MD, PhD, FRUUU, WEEE, OED

24

Because that's what the shiny stranger called himself – Dr. P'Klawz.

(In fact his real name was Sylvester Pearlyclaws. But he was in hiding because he had done so many terrible things that every police force on Earth was looking for him.)

And if anyone said the doctor had an Unusual name, which sounded like trying to put a crow into a sleeping bag, he would stare very hard at them until they cried.

As he went around the village, P'Klawz made sure to worry everyone he met and make them scared of Unusualness.

P'Klawz asked the postman, "Have you been bitten by any *Unusual* cats?" The postman said that he had never been bitten by any cats, although he had started to worry about it. Dr. P'Klawz warned him about cat bites every time they met. P'Klawz told him, "You should worry all the time. Unusual cats can hide in bread boxes, or under your bed, or anywhere. BUT FEAR NOT!" He yelled this last bit, so that the postman – who was a nervous person – jumped and dropped his mailbag. "I, Doctor P'Klawz, the Unusualness expert, will assist you! Take a leaflet."

"I have a leaflet."

"TAKE ANOTHER! YOU MIGHT LOSE IT!"

The postman ran home to his own ginger cat, who was called Jemima. "Oh, Jemima…" the postman whispered, "I hope you don't get Unusual. I don't think you'd fit in the bread box."

Jemima was a rather large cat. This was because her two hobbies were sleeping and eating the postman's butter when he forgot to put the lid back on the butter dish. The postman had never noticed.

Next, P'Klawz gave Hughie's mother a (very big) business card that listed various types of Unusualness for anyone silly enough to read it.

UNUSUALNESS!!!

TRUST THE WORLD-FAMOUS

DR. P'KLAWZ

HE CAN CURE ALL YOUR
UNUSUALNESS PROBLEMS:

- A BIT OF UNUSUALNESS
- MODERATE UNUSUALNESS
- CREEPING UNUSUALNESS
- HIGHLY UNUSUAL UNUSUALNESS
- EXTREME UNUSUALNESS

and even...

- PAJIMMINY-CRIMMINY UNUSUALNESS

P'KLAWZ CURES IT ALL!

EVERY TYPE OF UNUSUALNESS
SQUISHED UNTIL IT IS
NOTHINGNESS!!

UNUSUAL WIG

This made Hughie's mum wonder if maybe Hughie saying that he was a spaceman was a sign of Unusualness.

After that, Dr. P'Klawz made the Pandrumdroochit School headmaster worry that his wig might turn Unusual and start waving signals to the naughty boys at the back of the class. (This was almost true – the headmaster's wig did wave a little bit in strong winds and this made the naughty boys giggle.)

Once he had made lots of people less happy, P'Klawz went back to the little office he was renting beside the Pandrumdroochit Fire Station and stepped inside. Then he went and stood in front of his big mirror.

He practiced his smiling.

He never did seem to be able to make himself smile as if he was happy. This was because Dr. P'Klawz hated even the idea of being happy. Happiness made his teeth grind against each other and make a *skreee* noise, which hurt his ears and made his brain wriggle.

Then he practiced looking like a real doctor. (He wasn't a real doctor.)

This made him look frightening.

Then he practiced looking like Dr. P'Klawz. (Which, of course, wasn't his name.)

That made his face so scary we won't even think about it.

Away behind the Droochit Hills, Dr. P'Klawz had bought an old flour mill – which had once made lots of people happy, because you can make all kinds of cakes and scones out of flour. P'Klawz had paid people (not very much) to build a long, high fence all around the mill and then fill the place with maximum-security dormitories holding rattly metal beds to give people bad dreams. And even worse than this, he paid guards to paint the walls of the mill with these words: **THE P'KLAWZ INSTITUTION FOR MAXIMUM SECURITY AND UNUSUALNESS CURING**.

And P'Klawz had filled the big, nasty building with inmates – that was what he called all the people he had persuaded to come and be cured of

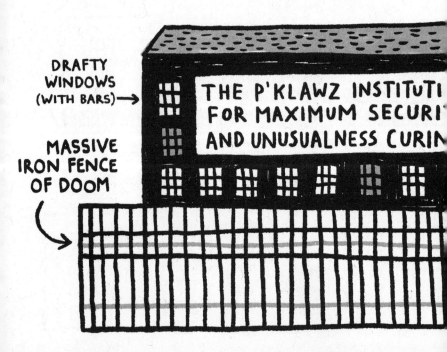

DRAFTY WINDOWS (WITH BARS)→

MASSIVE IRON FENCE OF DOOM

THE P'KLAWZ INSTITUTI FOR MAXIMUM SECURI AND UNUSUALNESS CURIN

Unusualness, and the people who had been sent by their friends and relatives after P'Klawz had persuaded them. He was a horrible person.

BIG TOWER

LOOMING GATES OF DOOM

P'Klawz also made the guards sweep every corner of every room in the Institution so that spiders could never build their webs there. He was afraid of spiders – he thought that having eight legs was Too Unusual. And he didn't like their webs, because they were Unusually Beautiful.

UNUSUALNESS AND LEGS - A HANDY GUIDE

← 8 LEGS TOO UNUSUAL

2 LEGS USUAL   4 LEGS FAIRLY USUAL   17 LEGS PAJIMMINY-CRIMMINY UNUSUAL!

And in his vest pocket, P'Klawz kept a shiny broken pocket watch that he could twirl and twirl and make people do whatever he wanted.

He wanted them to be unhappy.

SHY BADGER DANCING

SECTION FIVE

In which there is some lemonade and a leaflet. There is also some handy information about how important it is for llamas to have pretty fur if they would like to. And where is Uncle Shawn? Because there are some Highly Unusual things happening.

Back on the farm, Bill carried a fresh bucket of lemonade over to the llamas' drinking trough all by himself. At least, he thought he was by himself.

There was no one to be seen.

But Bill was certain he could hear two little feet tiptoeing whenever he took a step. It was almost as if he was being followed by Someone Invisible.

"Unusual..." thought Bill.

Bill had been thinking about Unusualness a lot lately, because of all the leaflets about it that came to the farmhouse mailbox. And now he was hearing invisible people. "The leaflets said Unusualness spreads faster than raindrops down weasels," Bill thought. "And Guinevere Llama will only eat square food – even though her favorite food is grapes and cheese balls and pancakes." Bill liked cooking and baking. But he didn't like cooking and baking all the time with no one to help him, especially when he had to make everything square.

"And Brian Llama wakes me up at night and says he can hear swamp monsters, or giant hungry owls, or extremely suspicious silences. And Carlos Llama makes fun of my legs sometimes and says they are short and fat – when they are elegant and just right for a badger who enjoys dancing." Bill loved dancing – especially to "This Badger's Gotta

SQUARE FOOD

SQUARE PIZZA

SQUARE FRIED EGGS

SQUARE SWISS ROLL

?

NOT SQUARE

CHEESE BALLS

PANCAKES, NOT SQUARE EITHER

ALSO NOT SQUARE

GRAPES

GUINEVERE'S FAVORITE FOOD

Move." He was shy, though, so he only danced in his bedroom where no one could watch.

"And Ginalolobrigida needs whole cupboards full of special combs and brushes and straighteners and curlers to make her fur absolutely perfect." It was extremely important for Ginalolobrigida Llama to look perfect.

Bill had asked her, "Why do you need straighteners *and* curlers? How can you tell which bits of fur should be straight and which bits of fur should be curly? Aren't the straight bits straight and the curly bits curly already?"

Ginalolobrigida made an unimpressed llama type of *huff* noise down her nose. "In the first place, I do not have *bits of fur*. And, of course, I cannot *just leave it alone* because I DO NOT WANT TO LOOK LIKE AN ANIMAL. I must look perfect."

Bill was beginning to think this was all Highly Unusual. 🐾

JAM SANDWICH

SECTION SIX

In which – finally! – Uncle Shawn is here! Also in this section are some firemen and jam sandwiches. But there is also an amount of Unusualness. Oh dear... This is quite a sad section.

Uncle Shawn was running up Pandrumdroochit's main street, throwing jam sandwiches and waving his arms like long socks in a washing machine, and shouting, "Left a bit! Up a bit! Sideways a bit! Get ready, everyone!"

Uncle Shawn's big mahogany shoes clattered on the pavement and his strange wiggly hair danced about, as if it were listening to music – possibly

37

"This Badger's Gotta Move," which is exactly the sort of tune to make anyone's hair dance.

The people in the village were used to Uncle Shawn acting in ways they didn't expect. Usually, they would have waved, or stood in their doorways and called, "Hello, Uncle Shawn! Isn't this a perfect day to be doing whatever peculiar thing it is that you're doing!"

But everyone in the village was worrying about Unusualness now. Nobody quite knew when they might look in their broom closet, or their garden

Pandrumdroochit
TARTAN & SOUVENIRS

shed, or their bathroom and see Dr. P'Klawz standing there with a new leaflet about Unusualness, or a lecture about how they might be Unusual themselves. The village school was very quiet because lots of the schoolchildren had seemed Unusual. (Children are full of all kinds of marvelous things, including Unusualness.) Most of them had been sent to P'Klawz's Institution. Some of their parents and uncles and cousins had gone there, too.

39

When the villagers saw Uncle Shawn throwing jam sandwiches and running about and shouting and laughing a lot, this seemed Extremely Unusual. So as Uncle Shawn passed by, everyone pretended he wasn't there.

Uncle Shawn, whose clever blue eyes never missed anything, said to himself, "Hmm. The shop that sells toffee has a CLOSED sign on the front door, even though it should be OPEN. And Mrs. McGuddlekiddy is watching me through her mail slot, as if I am a tiger... Something has happened to make everyone afraid." His hair wiggled, as if it was thinking.

The firemen of Pandrumdroochit weren't afraid. They hadn't read any leaflets, or listened as P'Klawz lectured them. They'd been busy doing firemen things and practicing so that they would be very fast and strong when anybody needed helping.

When Fire Chief Strachan heard the clatter of Uncle Shawn's big mahogany shoes, he cried, "It's

Uncle Shawn!" and everybody ran
to the fire station windows. The
firemen all waved and cheered,
"Hello, Uncle Shawn! How are
you?" This was much more like
the fun Uncle Shawn was used
to having in Pandrumdroochit.

Uncle Shawn threw some sandwiches in through
the windows and the firemen caught them. Jam
sandwiches were exactly the right things to go with
their mugs of tea after a hard morning spent getting
Reverend Peabody's head unstuck from between
some railings. "Hurray! Thank you, Uncle Shawn!"

Next door, the man who was calling himself
Dr. P'Klawz (but who was fibbing) was gritting
his big gleaming teeth. Ever since he was a child,
he had felt sick if anyone giggled and got itchy
skin if someone was playing hopscotch and really
enjoying it. As he had grown older, he had become
allergic to happiness, so he had decided to devote

41

his life to removing it from everyone he met. He had learned that if he made his voice sound smooth and strong, people would let him make them unhappy and steal the Unusualness inside them, which was there to make them just exactly themselves. And if he called himself Professor, or Captain, or Doctor, people trusted P'Klawz even more.

P'Klawz peered out of his window, just as Uncle Shawn dashed by and threw another sandwich. It was an especially sticky sandwich made with bramble jam and when it hit the window's glass, it stuck and then slowly slid downward, leaving a wide, brambly smear. Just for a moment, before he galloped past, Uncle Shawn saw a furious face staring at him through the stickiness and heard the sound of teeth squeaking.

Skreeeeee.

They squeaked like a cinema full of mice complaining about a very bad film with not enough adventures in it and no cheese.

THINGS THAT A CINEMA FULL OF MICE LIKE TO SEE IN FILMS:

① ADVENTURES

② CHEESE

SQUEAK SQUEAK

③ SQUEAKING

THINGS THAT A CINEMA FULL OF MICE DON'T LIKE TO SEE IN FILMS:

① CATS

② MORE CATS

③ CATS ON A MOTORBIKE

In that moment, Uncle Shawn felt as if he might be afraid. "Hmmm... Someone with a face that angry and teeth that loud might be a person who could frighten a whole village," he thought. "And that wouldn't be right at all." 🐾

VERY SCARED

SECTION SEVEN

In which some Extremely Unusual things

happen on Uncle Shawn's farm. And Brian has

to be brave again – and doesn't exactly manage.

And Carlos and Guinevere meet a pirate who

isn't really a pirate. If you are nervous, you

can read this bit holding someone's hand.

As long as their hand is not mysterious.

Brian Llama was standing in a corner of his barn
and feeling scared all over. The particular patch
of thin air he was staring at had just sneezed.
Before that, he had heard a pair of feet walking
– *pat, pat, pat* – across the soft sawdust on the

barn's floor, exactly as if Someone Invisible was inside the barn with him.

"Hello? Hello? *Hola??*" said Brian. "Are you a ghost? Please don't be a ghost. Ghosts are the worst. Except for swamp monsters." Brian couldn't help imagining the scariest things. "Or are you a giant invisible owl that wants to eat me?"

There was no answer.

A SPOTTER'S GUIDE TO INVISIBLE THINGS

INVISIBLE GHOST — INVISIBLE SWAMP MONSTER — GIANT INVISIBLE OWL — NOTHING

Brian stood ever so still for a long time; almost long enough for him to forget why. He even started to think that he might go to find Bill and ask him for some sultana scones with jam on top and some hot chocolate. It was exhausting being terrified, so he was really hungry.

"Maybe I was only imagining things." He waited a little bit longer. "I am glad there is not a giant invisible owl standing beside me, or an invisible swamp monster getting ready to eat me," said Brian to himself. "I'm glad no one with invisible arms is going to reach out for me with invisible fingers and—"

Brian didn't get the chance to finish saying "and touch me," because right then invisible tickly fingers did reach up and touch one of his ears very gently, as if they were saying hello.

"*Waaaaaaaaaaaaaaaaaaaaaaaaaaaaaaah!*" yelled Brian. "*EMERGENCIA!!!*" And he kept on yelling while he ran out of the barn even faster than Augusto Llama, the famous Peruvian Champion Llama Sprinter.

"EMERGENCIAAAAAAGH!!!"

Brian went on galloping until he was on the veranda of the farmhouse and then inside the farmhouse, up the stairs and in Bill's bedroom, hiding under Bill's bed.

Llamas don't really fit under beds. Brian knew that his legs were sticking out and that Someone Invisible might tickle his hooves at any time. So he decided to borrow Badger Bill's quilt with the pictures of famous badger explorers on it and put it over himself and stand very still, pretending to be a table with four llama-looking legs.

But a table in a bedroom would seem suspicious. So Brian went downstairs and hid in the living room and tried to look exactly like furniture and stop his knees from trembling.

This was Unusual.

PRETENDING TO BE A TABLE

Back in the llama barn, there was the sound of another sneeze – *schffew* – just as if Someone Invisible had got sawdust tickling his or her nose. Then there was a little sigh, just as if Someone Invisible had stroked a nice llama called Brian's ear to say hello, but then he had just yelled and run away.

Then there was the sound of Someone Invisible sitting down and sighing again.

I'm sure you will agree this was Unusual.

Meanwhile, Carlos Llama and Guinevere Llama were out in the llama meadow by the woods. Unfortunately, Guinevere had just nibbled a large and very delicious flower that Carlos thought was his favorite. This meant they were now having a llama argument. Llamas are quite fond of arguing – they do it instead of jumping rope or climbing trees, because they are not good at twirling jump ropes with their hooves and because a llama in a tree would look Highly Unusual.

"That was my flower!" shouted Carlos.

"Mmm-nnn-gngn," said Guinevere, eating the flower all the way down to the ground so that there was nothing left. "Yum."

"It was MINE!"

"It was delicious." Guinevere grinned. She liked teasing Carlos.

"It was called Juan and it was my favorite, and now you have eaten Juan all up, YOU GREEDY, FAT LLAMA!"

No one should ever tell a llama they are fat.

"FAT! Who are you calling fat, you horrible, cross-eyed, bandy-hooved bag of stupid fur!?!" shouted Guinevere, outraged.

You also should never say any of that to any llama. It will hurt their feelings.

"You've eaten my flower because you are THE WORST LLAMA IN THE WORLD. I HATE YOU!" yelled Carlos.

At this point Guinevere was about to tell Carlos that he was even uglier than Ugly Count Mefisto Llama, the very hideous and wicked llama that clever llama mothers made up to frighten llama children who aren't behaving themselves.

STICK FOR POKING THE TOOTH FAIRY

UGLY COUNT MEFISTO LLAMA

THE MOUSTACHE OF FEAR

BAG FOR TAKING AWAY TREATS

But Guinevere didn't say anything, because at that very moment, swinging down from a tree, came a small person wearing raggedy shorts and a raggedy shirt, a tweed mask and a pirate hat made out of newspaper. "Halt!" the small person commanded. "Stand your ground and I shall fight thee! Avast and shiver my timbers!"

"A vast what?" asked Guinevere, confused.

"A vast llama with a huge, wobbly bottom," muttered Carlos.

At this, the small person drew out of his belt a sword made from two bits of stick tied together with shoelaces. "Unhand that wonderful maiden, sir!"

"Wonderful maiden. Phaw!" sniggered Carlos. Guinevere kicked him in the leg. "Ow!"

"Fear not, pretty damsel. I will protect thee!" bellowed the little person from behind his mask.

"She is not a damsel, she is a llama," replied Carlos. "And who are you?"

"Yes, who are you?" asked Guinevere. "Because I really don't need you to defend me." She kicked Carlos again when he wasn't looking. "Although you must be a very clever person, because you have realized that I am wonderful." She smiled at the small person and his odd mask, which didn't fit his face very well and was patched together out of different bits of scratchy tweed cloth.

"I am the Famous Tweed-Faced Boy!" announced the small person, waggling his sword about so wildly that he twanged Guinevere's nose with it.

"Ouch!" said Guinevere. "I have never heard of you, so you can't be famous. Please stop waving your pretend shoelaces sword."

THE FAMOUS TWEED-FACED BOY

At this, the small boy – because he was a small boy behind his mask and under his newspaper hat – said, more quietly, "When I grow up, I am going to be a famous pirate. And then I will get a real pirate hat that isn't made of newspaper and a real pirate ship and I will fill it with treasure and then—"

Carlos made a *huff* noise down his long llama nose and said, "You are far too tiny to be a pirate, and that mask and that hat make you look like an idiot."

But then the Tweed-Faced Boy started to cry. And while he snuffled, he shouted, "I'm big for my age and I'm brave, and I have to get treasure and a ship because I need to find my sister and you don't understand anything!"

Before either of the llamas could stop him, he ran back into the woods, climbed up into a tree and swung away along the branches until he was out of sight.

"What an Unusual person," said Carlos.

"Yes," said Guinevere. "He is perhaps full of the Unusualness that is mentioned in those silly leaflets we keep finding nailed to our barn door. Perhaps we should wash our hooves in case we catch Unusualness."

"Yes, let's do that," agreed Carlos. And as they walked towards the llama-bathing barn, he said, "What were we fighting about?"

"I don't remember."

"Oh well. We can be friends again," said Carlos. As they walked, he noticed a flower growing. "Ah, there is my favorite flower." He trotted over and sniffed a tall flower growing out of the grass and looking proud of itself. "He's called Juan."

JUAN THE FLOWER

"I thought the one I just ate was called Juan."

NOT JUAN THE FLOWER

"You just ate Juan!?!"

"You don't even know which flower is Juan!"

"This one is Juan!"

"One is one? Which one is Juan?" Guinevere sniggered.

"Oh, you are an annoying llama!"

"I am sure Juan doesn't like having your big, wet nose vacuuming up all his scent."

"If anyone has a big nose, it's you – BIG NOSE!" yelled Carlos.

And within seconds, they were busy fighting each other and had forgotten about the Tweed-Faced Boy and his quest to find his sister. 🐾

UNUSUALLY TASTY APPLE CRUMBLE

SECTION EIGHT

In which Bill meets some new Unusualness. And then he decides to visit somewhere that he really, really shouldn't and no matter how loudly we shout at this book, he won't hear us saying that he should just go home and have some bread and honey instead. If only Uncle Shawn could help... But will he be able to? Will defeating P'Klawz be too much for him? We can hardly bear to think about it.

While all this Unusualness was happening to the llamas, Badger Bill was walking along the seashore. He really wanted to tell someone a joke, but Uncle Shawn was nowhere to be seen. So Bill

57

said out loud to the breeze, "What's the difference between a piano and a fish?"

There was no answer.

Bill asked the sand the same question, but the sand didn't say anything, either.

Then he walked down to the very edge of the water, near where Uncle Shawn had been making his Unusual noises and patting the water. Bill asked again, "What's the difference between a piano and a fish?"

There was no reply. But just as Bill turned round to begin walking back to the farmhouse, he heard a very deep, bubbly, watery voice say, very slowly, **"YOOOU CAAAN TUUUNE A PIANOOO. BUT YOOOU CAAAN'T TUUUNAAA FIIISH."**

Bill looked down at the water and caught sight of two very enormous and clever eyes peering up at him. One of the eyes winked.

While he ran away as fast as a badger with short

VERY FAST (for short legs)

but elegant dancer's legs can run, Bill thought to himself, "I really am a very brave badger. But eyes in the sea – that's Too Unusual for me!"

And he kept on running.

By the time Bill stopped, he realized that he was in the village of Pandrumdroochit.

"I wonder if Uncle Shawn patting the sea has made it Unusual?" thought Bill. "Oh no – that means he might be suffering from really bad Unusualness... What shall I do?"

And then Bill noticed the shiny sign that Dr. P'Klawz (who wasn't really called P'Klawz and wasn't really a doctor and who was just a big fibber with a nice suit) had put outside his office.

It said:

ARE YOU FEELING breathless AND worried? HAVE YOUR FRIENDS CAUGHT UNUSUALNESS? FEAR NOT! → DR. P'KLAWZ ← (WHO IS ABSOLUTELY A REAL DOCTOR AND NOT A BIG FIBBER) CAN CURE ALL UNUSUALNESS AND SQUISH IT INTO NOTHINGNESS!!! (FOR A SMALL FEE)

pandrumdroochit

Bill couldn't remember seeing the sign before. But maybe if the famous Dr. P'Klawz was right here, he could help Bill find out if everyone at the llama farm was suffering from Unusualness.

Bill put out his paw and opened the door...

Elsewhere in the village of Pandrumdroochit, Uncle Shawn was in Mrs. MacDonald's garden, crunching a toffee. (It was covered in sand from his pocket.) He was sitting in an apple tree, next to Mrs. MacDonald's cat, Bob. Mrs. MacDonald looked up at them both. "He knows how to climb down, he just doesn't want to," she said.

"Yes." Uncle Shawn nodded, tickling the cat's tummy. "He likes company and he especially likes firemen, don't you, Bob? That's why you pretend to be stuck, so the firemen have to come and rescue you." Bob purred but admitted nothing. Uncle Shawn waved a jam sandwich at Mrs. MacDonald happily. "Would you like half of my last sandwich?"

"No, no. I'll go and call the firemen. Would you like some tea with that?"

"Yes, please," said Uncle Shawn. He swung his feet in the air and enjoyed the view. From up here, he could see all the way to the sea and the llama farm.

At that moment, P'Klawz popped up from behind a rosebush. (He had sneaked all the way there from his office.) "There is no time for tea! Behold! I am the world-famous Unusualness doctor! I am Doctor P'Klawz!"

"You're Doctor Pickles?" asked Mrs. MacDonald – she'd never met him before, because she didn't go out much. "I don't really like pickles, they disagree with me."

"Not *Pickles!*" snapped Dr. P'Klawz. Then he remembered he was trying

62

to seem nice and he smiled like sunbeams rattling around in a freshly scrubbed toilet. "I am Doctor P'Klawz. Allow me to show you the leaflet I pushed through your mail slot earlier. I think you will find that you didn't read it carefully enough."

"I didn't read it at all. There are leaflets coming through my mail slot all the time just now. I use them to light the fire."

"Do you realize how dangerous that might be?"

"No, I'm very good at lighting fires. I've been doing it for years."

"I mean it is dangerous not to read my leaflets!"

"Well, I have been quite busy."

"PANDRUMDROOCHIT IS TURNING UNUSUAL!"

"Pandrumdroochit is a very happy village," said Mrs. MacDonald. "Sometimes visitors come to our tearoom and fall asleep before they can have their tea because it's so peaceful."

P'Klawz made his voice sound as soothing as

honey and lemon. "You are a busy lady and have no time to think, so I will think for you. Up in your tree, you have a cat who will not obey you. That is Unusual."

"No, it's not," called Uncle Shawn, who was studying Dr. P'Klawz very carefully with his clever blue eyes. He grinned. "Cats never obey people, because they have plans that human people don't know about."

"Then how do you know? You're people," said Dr. P'Klawz, being very sly. But he started to scratch his ears and elbows and bottom, because Uncle Shawn's happiness was making his skin itch. P'Klawz murmured to Mrs. MacDonald, "You have an Unusual man talking to your Unusual cat. No one should ever talk to cats, because they cannot answer. And that man—"

"They answer if you listen. I'm Uncle Shawn. Hello, Mr. Pickles."

"It's *P'Klawz. Doctor P'Klawz*," Dr. P'Klawz lied. Then he smiled like a whole warehouse full of lavatories and threw Uncle Shawn a shiny white card that said: DR. P'KLAWZ – CALL AT ONCE IN CASE OF UNUSUALNESS.

P'Klawz gave Mrs. MacDonald a card, too, and said sneakily to her, "That Uncle Shawn is sitting in a tree. Grown-ups must never sit in trees. It is far too Unusual."

"But it's fun," said Uncle Shawn. "And I am not a grown-up. I decided when I was a boy that I would never turn into a grown-up and I never have.

65

I am just a tall human person." Uncle Shawn swung his feet in his big mahogany shoes in front of Dr. P'Klawz's grinding teeth.

"You're meant to be grown-up and miserable! You are not supposed to throw jam sandwiches at people's windows!" shouted P'Klawz. "You are not supposed to climb trees or have fun! YOU ARE COMPLETELY UNUSUAL!"

"Thank you." Uncle Shawn smiled. "I try my best." And he stared at Dr. P'Klawz as if he was thinking that his jam sandwich was more likely to be a real doctor than P'Klawz. Uncle Shawn was very clever at knowing people.

① REAL DOCTOR   ② JAM SANDWICH   ③ DR. P'KLAWZ

66

Uncle Shawn's general happiness was making P'Klawz's teeth *skreeeee* as loud as a large man on a tiny bicycle with rusty brakes. "You must be treated immediately – *skreeeeee* – for all your terrible Unusualness before it spreads to everybody else!"

"Spreads like fun and happiness, you mean?" asked Uncle Shawn gently.

"*Skreeeeeeeeeeeeeeeeeeee!*" said P'Klawz's teeth. "You need locking up until you are miserable and then locking up some more!"

And then he remembered that Mrs. MacDonald was listening and whispered sweetly to her, "We only lock all the doors and windows in my Institution to keep out drafts." (This was a very big fib.)

P'Klawz took out his pocket watch and made it spin. "This is my Unusualness detector." (This was a fib.) "Look at how it is shining…" The watch sparkled and sprookled so much that it dazzled Mrs. MacDonald and made her thinking fuzzy.

"That's just a broken old watch," Uncle Shawn pointed out.

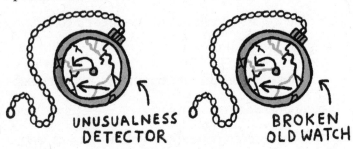

UNUSUALNESS DETECTOR

BROKEN OLD WATCH

P'Klawz purred to Mrs. MacDonald, "Allow me, gentle lady, to escort you indoors away from all this Unusualness. A normal, usual person can catch Unusualness from an Unusual person, so you shouldn't ever go near one. And you certainly shouldn't let one sit in your tree. Probably you should cut the tree down and saw it into little bits and burn them."

"But it's my favorite apple tree," said Mrs. MacDonald. "My grandfather planted it and it gives me wonderful apples every year."

68

"Are they Unusual apples?" asked P'Klawz, and his eyes glittered.

"They are Unusually Tasty and Juicy."

"Then they should be burned, too."

"I normally make them into pies and crumbles. I give some to the firemen."

"You must set fire to the Unusual apples and crumbles. Then bury them," Dr. P'Klawz said soothingly. He shooed Mrs. MacDonald away from the tree and watched her go inside. Then he hissed up at Uncle Shawn, "Soon no one will want to see you and your Unusual clothes and your Unusual hair and your Unusual shoes and your Unusual face. They won't want to be your friend anymore. Someone as Unusual as you shouldn't have any friends."

This made Uncle Shawn's blue eyes even bluer while he thought a lot and decided things. "You are not a nice man," he said. "And I do not think you are a doctor."

"Shall I tell you a secret?" asked Dr. P'Klawz.

"Oh, I love secrets, yes," said Uncle Shawn.

Dr. P'Klawz made his voice into a shivery, cold whisper and told Uncle Shawn, "You are right. I am not nice at all and I hate you, Uncle Shawn. Everywhere I have gone, everyone has told me that you are the happiest man they have ever met."

"That's nice to know." Uncle Shawn smiled.

Dr. P'Klawz's pointy, pinky nose sniffled the air. "You even smell like happiness. And you're exactly like yourself and nobody else, and that's what makes you happy all over and it must be stopped! One way or another I will squish the happiness and Unusualness right out of you."

"That's horrible," said Uncle Shawn.

"I know! It's wonderfully horrible, isn't it?" said Dr. P'Klawz, and he made a noise like very old swamp monsters wheezing, which was what he did instead of laughing. "In the end, this whole country will be free from happiness. No fun, no laughter. No singing. No dances. No whistling. NO UNUSUALNESS."

Uncle Shawn quietly asked, "Are you sure that you'll like what you get in the end?" Because he always wanted to give people the chance to change their minds when they were doing something silly. "If there is no happiness anywhere, then you won't be happy yourself, you know..."

But P'Klawz grinned like a whole showroom of bathtubs. "Everyone will be exactly the same and everyone will be miserable, and my skin will stop itching and my ears will be comfortable and my teeth will be quiet and my head won't ache. And whenever I feel sad, I will think that you have no friends anymore and that without your Unusualness you will be nobody at all, and that will make me laugh and laugh."

Uncle Shawn rubbed at his wibbly wobbly hair to make himself feel brave. "Ha! Well, you shouldn't have told me all that, because now I will tell everyone the truth about you and they will stop reading your leaflets, and they will have extra fun, just to annoy you."

"Nobody will even listen to you, because nobody is speaking to you. They will just ignore you. Because you are Too Unusual." And P'Klawz made a noise like someone scraping a pebble along sandpaper. This was what he did instead of giggling. Then he stepped neatly away – *tip, tip, tip* – on his very shiny shoes, under his very shiny hair that looked like paint.

This left Uncle Shawn with Bob the cat. After a while, when the firemen didn't arrive – because Mrs. MacDonald hadn't called them – Bob got bored and climbed down from the tree all by himself. He went to sleep on the roof of the shed in a patch of sunshine.

Uncle Shawn swung his feet and thought big thoughts about Dr. P'Klawz. "It's not right for this pretend doctor to frighten people and make them sad. And I do not like the sound of his Institution, not one teeny tiny bit."

At that very moment, a huge gray van went past. On its side – in darker gray letters – was painted: **INSTITUTION FOR MAXIMUM SECURITY AND UNUSUALNESS CURING – COLLECTION SERVICE**.

Peering out of its tiny, barred window was Hughie, the little boy who wanted to be a spaceman. P'Klawz had hypnotized Hughie's mum to make her send Hughie to the Institution to cure him of his Unusualness. But really P'Klawz just wanted to squish all the fun out of him so that he would end up as gray as the van he was being taken away in. Hughie's face looked very sad, even when Uncle Shawn waved and smiled.

INSTITUTION FOR MAXIMUM SECURITY AND UNUSUALNESS CURING-COLLECTION SERVICE

"Well now. This all needs fixing, doesn't it?" said Uncle Shawn. He felt nervous in his tummy. "I think I have a plan, but it is a scary plan... Oh dear."

SECTION NINE

In which we learn about goats. And Bill

still has a table with very hairy legs.

Back at the llama farm, Brian was still pretending to be a table. Guinevere and Carlos were fighting in the meadow, shouting and kicking up dust with their hooves until they looked like a big noisy cloud with two pairs of llama ears sticking out of it.

But Ginalolobrigida Llama was having a delightful afternoon. Her new hoof polish was glistening and she could tell she was looking especially lovely.

She was about to begin putting on her makeup for the day (Ginalolobrigida sometimes got up very late, because being so gorgeous was tiring) when she heard a sigh. It was such a sad noise that she turned round and looked to see who could be unhappy when they were lucky enough to be in the same barn as probably the loveliest llama in the world.

"Hello?" she said. All she got in reply was another, sadder sigh from a patch of thin air. Ginalolobrigida had heard of people who were shy and she knew that shy people didn't like being looked at. "Hello? Are you shy? Have you turned invisible because you are shy?"

Ginalolobrigida waited. There was silence.

"Are you one of those unfortunate people who don't like to appear in public, or wear magnificent hats, or dance the famous Peruvian chicha dance in front of admiring crowds?"

Ginalolobrigida was sure someone was there, because she could hear breathing. "Well, if you won't speak, you might as well not be here," said

Ginalolobrigida, and she started applying her Hot Llama Lavender lipstick.

GINALOLOBRIGIDA

PERUVIAN PERM POWDER

TRENDY BENDY CURLING IRONS

JUANITA LLAMA BRAND HOOF POLISH

NOSE BLUSHER

HOT LLAMA LAVENDER LIPSTICK

SMOOTHING PADS ↓

LEG BRUSH

EAR COMB

EMERGENCY PANCAKE

TWEAKERS

TWEEZERS

MAKEUP BRUSHES

77

Her makeup brushes started rattling, as if little hands were searching through them. Ginalolobrigida watched while her tweezers and tweakers and curling irons and smoothing pads and pot of nose blusher and all the rest rattled, too. Some of her makeup pots even floated into the air, just as if an Invisible Someone with little hands and fingers was lifting them to read their labels. Finally a small voice asked, "What are these for?"

"Well," said Ginalolobrigida, "they help me feel as lovely as I want to."

"Why?" said the voice – which sounded like a little girl who happened to be invisible.

"Because it's nice to feel lovely," said Ginalolobrigida. She wasn't at all scared. If this invisible person was interested in makeup, then she must be nice and very sensible. "Have you been shy for long?"

"I'm not shy. I'm a ghost. *Wooo-ooo,*" said the voice, trying to be frightening.

Ginalolobrigida only really got frightened when she ran out of eyeliner. Or pancakes. "Are you sure you're a ghost? Ghosts smell terrible and have long, scratching horns and funny little eyes and beards."

"That's *goats*," explained the voice. "*Ghosts* are scary spirits that make things go bump in the night. And they howl. *Wooo-ooo*."

THE DIFFERENCE BETWEEN GHOSTS AND GOATS

1. HOWL
2. MAKE THINGS GO BUMP IN THE NIGHT
3. SCARY

1. BLEAT
2. EAT ALMOST ANYTHING
3. A BIT SCARY

"Well, if you really are a ghost, you're not good at it because I'm not even a little bit terrified."

"Oh," said the Invisible Someone's voice.

She sounded so unhappy that Ginalolobrigida felt sorry for her. "Would you like to try some of my lipstick? Do you have lips?"

There was another sigh. "I used to. I used to like talking to squirrels and waving at strangers, only everyone said that was Unusual and I got sent to an Institution run by a horrible doctor with loud teeth. Every night I wished very hard to be invisible so I could escape. I knew that no one notices quiet people who are empty inside. So I was as quiet as sleeping mice and I felt very empty because I missed my mum and dad. And my brother most – we're twins... And I disappeared."

"How long have you been invisible?"

"Oh, for ages and ages," grumbled the little voice. "Now when I talk to people, or try to play with them, they scream. So I decided I might actually try to be frightening. But you're not frightened. Oh dear, life is terrible..."

Ginalolobrigida thought life was generally

nice – as long as no one was trying to make her into pies, or prevent her from smelling of lavender – so she said, "Why don't I put some Velvety Violet Lip Liner on for you?"

"Well, it might be a bit more fun than following people around and stealing bits of their dinner when they're not looking..."

THINGS TO DO IF YOU ARE INVISIBLE

1. STEAL OTHER PEOPLE'S DINNER   2. MAKE FART NOISES NEXT TO IMPORTANT PEOPLE   3. PLAY CATCH UNTIL PEOPLE RUN AWAY

"That's the spirit." Ginalolobrigida knew that having just the right color of lips should cheer anybody up. "Now, this will be very difficult. Fortunately, I am a makeup genius. Let's begin."

And while that was happening, Guinevere and

81

Carlos fought – so that even the tips of their ears were not visible over the top of the dust cloud.

And while that was happening, Brian – his furry knees knocking – was still pretending to be a table.

Back in Pandrumdroochit, Uncle Shawn was walking past closed curtains and sad gardens full of bare patches, where Unusually Beautiful plants had been uprooted. No one spoke to him, or waved or smiled.

At last he came to the edge of the village, where there used to be a sign that said:

PANDRUMDROOCHIT
GOODBYE! PLEASE VISIT AGAIN.
WE LIKE YOU.

And on the other side of the sign it had said:

YOU ARE ENTERING
PANDRUMDROOCHIT.
WELCOME!

But someone had painted a new sign with dull brown letters. It now just said:

A usual village.
Nothing to see here.
GO AWAY.

On both sides.

"Hmmm," said Uncle Shawn to himself. "I suppose Doctor P'Klawz decided that

Pandrumdroochit was an Unusual name. Which is very silly, because P'Klawz is really a Very Unusual name... Perhaps a Pajimminy-Crimminy Unusual name." Uncle Shawn pondered for a moment. "I seem to remember someone with a name like P'Klawz. Someone Unusual... Hmmm..."

And he nearly – but not quite – remembered there was a master criminal called Sylvester Pearlyclaws.

Uncle Shawn thought, "I wish I could tell Bill about my plan for defeating P'Klawz, but I can't – even though Bill is my best friend ever. If he knows about it, then it won't work."

This made his feet feel sad as he headed for home. 🐾

SECTION TEN

*In which sneaky Dr. P'Klawz tells all kinds
of fibs to poor Bill and makes his paws go
wibbly, and things are looking very bad for
Bill and Uncle Shawn and the whole farm.*

Since arriving at Dr. P'Klawz's office, Bill had
looked at the big chart on the wall, which
showed the Stages of Unusualness. And he had
looked at the poster that warned against wearing Unusual socks, because they could distract
your toes and make you trip over things. And
he had just finished looking at the poster about
Unusual cats hiding in your bread box.

THE STAGES OF UNUSUALNESS

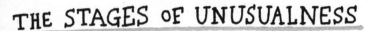

① VERY UNUSUAL

BEING DISOBEYED BY CATS

② HA HA! HA HA! HA!

ENJOYING JOKES

③ NEEDING TO EAT TOASTED CHEESE

④ HI

ATTRACTING SPIDERS

⑤ TOO UNUSUAL

HAVING FUN WITH FRIENDS

⑥ EXPLODING TOENAILS

⑦ LOSS OF ALL HAIR

⑧ HIGHLY UNUSUAL

CAN ONLY SAY THE WORD "BANANA"

"I never realized that Unusualness was such a problem. But I suppose it must be, because it's on a poster," thought Bill.

Then, because the office was warm and had soft chairs that weren't covered in pancake crumbs and llama fur and jam, Bill leaned back and fell fast asleep.

This meant that he was very surprised when Dr. P'Klawz came in and found him, snoring gently. (Sometimes creatures with beautifully large, stripy noses can't help snoring.)

"AH!" yelled Dr. P'Klawz. "A badger! On one of my chairs! Unusualness!"

Bill didn't wake quickly enough to see how very scared P'Klawz was by anything unexpected. Bill blinked and shook his ears and said, "No, I'm not the Unusual one."

"Ah! A talking badger! Highly Unusual!" P'Klawz clenched his teeth. "I am the great and wonderful P'Klawz. If you're not Unusual, why are you here? Have Unusual things been happening to you?"

"Ummm," said Bill. He didn't quite trust P'Klawz. "I might be worrying about nothing..."

"No, you should always worry about everything

FIBBING BATHTUB →

HELLO, I AM YOUR NEW GYM TEACHER AND DEFINITELY NOT A BATH.

– especially in the dark at night, when you are by yourself." P'Klawz smiled like a fibbing bathtub. "Are you a wealthy talking badger? Do you perform in circuses? Do you have extensive savings?"

"Not really," said Bill.

P'Klawz frowned. "Our full Unusualness Squishing is expensive. If a person you know is Unusual, we can try painting them all over with gray paint, which only costs five hundred pounds, but it very rarely works..." He waved his extremely clean pink fingers in a threatening way. "Unusualness can be costly."

"The llama farm doesn't make a lot of money," Bill explained. "We don't have many llamas and they like their fur so much that we only cut it when they are very hot in the summer. Sometimes we sell honey from the bees. Or Carlos goes to the village and gives lectures about Peruvian mountains... We're mostly just happy."

The doctor's teeth gave a small squeak.

"And we have fun."

The doctor's teeth gave a louder squeak. "Fun is a sure sign of Unusualness."

"Are you sure?" asked Bill. "I thought fun was a sign of more fun to come. And maybe laughing and mugs of cocoa."

The doctor shuddered. "You poor, deluded badger. You sound as if Unusualness is already seeping into your fur."

Bill remembered hearing footsteps when there

89

was nobody there, and the great big eyes and the great big voice that told him a joke from the sea. And the Unusual things Uncle Shawn did all the time. "Well... Mainly I was worried about Uncle Shawn."

Dr. P'Klawz's teeth squeaked like un-oiled wheelbarrows going down mountains. "Uncle Shawn! He is Pajimminy-Crimminy Unusual! I have never seen a worse case! He climbs trees! He's kind to cats! He has fun and enjoys it!"

This sounded to Bill like things he liked about Uncle Shawn. "Couldn't you just cure his Unusualness and leave all those other things because they're nice?"

"Nice!?!" P'Klawz said the word as if it tasted of earwax, or sour milk. "Nice!?! No one who isn't Highly Unusual wants to be anywhere near anything nice!"

Bill thought he didn't really like P'Klawz. He decided to leave. But before he could stand all the

HYPNOTIZED
BADGER

way up on his brave, not-too-short-for-a-badger legs, P'Klawz took out his pocket watch and twirled it in front of Bill's eyes. After a minute of staring at the shiny watch, Bill felt floppy and as if he wanted to do whatever P'Klawz suggested.

P'Klawz sniggered. This sounded like sad weasels sneezing. He picked up a long sheet of paper off his desk – it was covered in tiny writing. He offered it to Bill. "Here! Sign this!"

"Hmmmmm," said Bill, woozily. "What is it?"

"Oh, it just gives me permission to take Uncle Shawn to my Institution for Maximum Security and Unusualness Curing and squish the Unusualness out of him until he is completely flat. I won't even charge you! I'll squish him for free!"

Even though he was hypnotized, Bill felt worried in his big, kind badger heart. "Mmmmm... Is your Institution nice? Does it have fresh scones and pancakes for tea and happy views out of the windows and rocking chairs and cocoa?" His eyes felt woolly, but he wanted his friend to be safe with P'Klawz. "Uncle Shawn would need all those things. And peppermints."

"Just sign here," said the doctor, waving a pen in one hand and the sheet of paper in the other. "Sign the paper, Mr. Badger." He grinned like a fishmonger's slab.

Badger Bill managed to stand up and said, "I've changed my mind. We will all just stay as

92

THINGS THAT YOU CANNOT FIND
IN THE INSTITUTION FOR MAXIMUM
SECURITY AND UNUSUALNESS CURING

1. COCOA
2. FRESH SCONES
3. PANCAKES
4. ROCKING CHAIRS

THINGS THAT YOU CAN FIND
IN THE INSTITUTION FOR MAXIMUM
SECURITY AND UNUSUALNESS CURING

1. SQUISHED PEOPLE

we are, thanks." He tried to walk very quickly towards the door, even though his paws were hypnotized and stumbly. "I'll be off now. I have pancakes to make."

"You'll be sorry," purred Dr. P'Klawz into Bill's ear. "Unusualness always gets worse. In the end, even I won't be able to cure Uncle Shawn."

"Goodbye," Badger Bill managed to say, his paw on the doorknob, and then he tumbled outside and walked away as fast as he could manage.

"He's a nasty doctor," Bill said to himself, tugging at his whiskers and shaking his head so that he felt more steady. "Horrible." And he walked a bit faster, so that he was almost running. "I'll go straight home and have a mug of cocoa and relax. Probably everything will be fine when I get there."

SECTION ELEVEN

In which you should look away now if you are allergic to Unusualness. Maybe you should even hide under a table. As long as it really is a table...

Carlos and Guinevere had now been fighting for so long that they couldn't remember why and were very tired and thirsty, which made them even more bad-tempered and even more likely to shout "Big nose!" and maybe "Wobbly bottom!" at each other. The dust cloud they had kicked up was so thick they had no idea where they were anymore.

• • •

And at about that time, Ginalolobrigida had finished putting foundation and lip liner and lipstick and glitter gloss on her invisible new friend. She had also applied eyeliner and three shades of carefully blended eye shadow. Ginalolobrigida was so proud of her work that she decided to trot along to the farmhouse and show everyone. "Come along," she said to her friend. "What should I call you, by the way, little invisible girl?"

"Why not call me Linvizzygirl?" said the mouth and eyes that Ginalolobrigida's makeup skills had revealed.

"Don't you have a real name?"

"It's a secret." The mouth and eyes looked sad.

"Well," Ginalolobrigida continued, "now we must let everyone see I can even apply beautiful makeup to someone with an invisible face."

"Are you sure that people won't be worried when they see a mouth and two eyes floating in thin air in front of them?" asked Linvizzygirl, who

Friendly (invisible) Person

Worried (visible) Person

had been invisible for a while and knew that people (and llamas called Brian) got very frightened when they saw – or didn't see – things that were Unusual.

"No, no, no!" Ginalolobrigida laughed. "Everyone at this farm is far too sensible to be worried about that kind of thing. Come on.

97

We can have some pancakes while we're there – I'm sure Badger Bill will have made some. He's always making pancakes – he really enjoys it, so we let him do it a lot."

And they both went out of the barn together, happily making lists of pancakes they would like to eat.

GINALOLOBRIGIDA PANCAKES

LINVIZZYGIRL PANCAKES

TREE-SAP PANCAKES

STOLEN PLAIN PANCAKES AND ICE CREAM

RASPBERRY AND CLOVER PANCAKES

STOLEN PANCAKES WITH TOFFEE SAUCE

MINT, VANILLA AND POTATO PANCAKES

STOLEN BLUEBERRY PANCAKES

98

Meanwhile, Uncle Shawn was sitting by a table, thinking very hard – so hard that he didn't really notice anything else apart from the gargantunormous plan that he was hatching.

And Badger Bill was walking down the soft path to the farmhouse. He said to himself, "I will just have a nice sit down and a cookie. That will be lovely and peaceful." He needed some peace after being hypnotized.

As Bill reached the front door, he could hear something like thunder far away.

And then Bill opened the door and – goodness – he heard and tasted and smelled and saw lots of things all at once.

And they were all Unusual! They were all PAJIMMINY-CRIMMINY UNUSUAL!

There were hoofprints all over the hallway that he had only swept that morning. And the thunder was much louder and coming towards him...

When he opened the living room door he couldn't see anything except a thick, swirling cloud of dust. Then he realized the thunder wasn't thunder – it was the sound of llama hooves!

Guinevere and Carlos had fought right across the farm and up to the farmhouse, and then all the way indoors and into the living room. The whole room smelled of hot llama and farm dust.

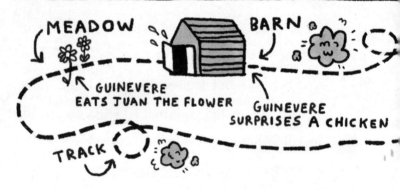

PLAN OF GUINEVERE AND CARLOS'S FIGHT

MEADOW   BARN

GUINEVERE EATS JUAN THE FLOWER

GUINEVERE SURPRISES A CHICKEN

TRACK

"What on earth is happening?" Bill said. Somebody kicked him in the shin and someone else yelled, "Crumply ears!" right into one of his not-at-all-crumply ears.

100

Bill peered very hard through the dust and he could just see ... a table with hairy llama legs!

Brian Llama was still hiding and still wearing Bill's favorite quilt – which was now all creased and covered in llama hair and layers and layers of dirt.

Brian was also yelling at the top of his voice, "*EMERGENCIA! Aaaaaaaaaaaaaaaaaaaaaaaaaa*

FIELD

STREAM

ORCHARD

CARLOS BITES A PASSING SHEEP BY MISTAKE

EVERYONE GETS RATHER WET

HILL

aaaaaaaaaaaaaaaaaaaaaaaaaaaaaaaaaaaaaaaaaaaaa aaaaaaaaaaaah! EMERGENCIA!" He thought that Carlos and Guinevere were a swamp monster with lots of feet. They definitely sounded like one.

101

Bill – who was now very, very annoyed – yelled, "EVERYBODY STOP! STOP DOING WHATEVER YOU ARE DOING! THIS IS ALL PAJIMMINY-CRIMMINY UNUSUAL!"

Everyone stood still – especially Brian – and didn't make a sound.

The dust began to settle so that the carpet started to look a bit like a llama-hairy beach, or a piece of furry desert.

And for a moment things seemed sensible.

Only then Ginalolobrigida Llama trotted happily in through the back door, followed by a floating mouth and a pair of eyes, and announced, "Look! Isn't this wonderful? I'm not only gorgeous, I'm a genius!"

Brian saw the floating eyes and mouth and screamed so loudly that all the glasses in the kitchen broke. "*EMERGENCIA!*"

And then in through the window climbed a small boy wearing a newspaper hat and a tweed mask who cried, "I am the Tweed-Faced Boy! I will save you!" and ran to help Brian, because he sounded like a damsel in distress.

Brian – who was scared of pirates (and small boys and tweed) – threw off Bill's quilt, which fell onto the hoofprinted, dusty floor. "Please, sir, I am not a damsel."

"You screamed like a damsel. Have you eaten a damsel?" shouted the Tweed-Faced Boy.

This frightened Brian so much that he ran into the kitchen and tried to hide under a dish towel.

A dish towel is a lot smaller than a llama. His nose stuck out. So did the whole of his body. And his legs.

DISH TOWEL (QUITE SMALL) + LLAMA (BIGGER) = !!!

The Tweed-Faced Boy went over to Brian and rubbed his tummy to see if there was a damsel inside him. This made Brian giggle.

Bill could see Uncle Shawn sitting quietly in his favorite armchair and smiling as if he was having a wonderful time. "Hello, Bill," said Uncle Shawn. "Are you having a nice day?"

"What!?!" said Bill, who suddenly felt very cross and peculiar. "How could I be having a nice day!?! Uncle Shawn – look at the mess! Look at my ruined quilt! Look at Brian getting llama fur on my only clean dish towel. Look at Guinevere nipping Carlos's ear!"

Guinevere stopped biting Carlos and both llamas tried to look innocent while Ginalolobrigida stuck her tongue out at them. Linvizzygirl's eyes and mouth giggled, and the Tweed-Faced Boy studied her from behind his mask and under his newspaper hat.

Uncle Shawn just sat and smiled even more.

"Oh, I'm sure that you can clear this up, all by yourself, without us helping you." He closed his eyes and whistled a little tune.

This made Bill even more furious. "I never make any mess!" he shouted. "Why am I always the badger who cleans up the mess!?"

"You're the only badger we have," said Uncle Shawn.

UNCLE SHAWN'S FAVORITE ARMCHAIR

WHISTLING A LITTLE TUNE

ANGRY BADGER

This made Bill angrier than a badger had ever been – even the famously bad-tempered Karl Badger, whose face was so red and hot from always yelling that other badgers would hold bread against his cheeks to make toast. This made Karl even more furious.

Karl Badger

Bill shouted so loud that his whiskers went straight, "And look at Ginalolobrigida!"

"Yes, everyone should always look at me," agreed Ginalolobrigida.

"You are standing right next to a floating mouth and eyes!" said Bill. "THIS IS TOO UNUSUAL!"

At this, Linvizzygirl's eyes started crying and her mouth said, "I'm not Unusual and you're all horrible – apart from this tall, furry lady with the makeup. I'm not staying!"

Everyone heard the sound of invisible feet stamping off, then the back door swung open and was slammed shut by an invisible hand.

"And who are you?" growled Bill to the small boy in the newspaper hat.

"I am the Tweed-Faced Boy!" announced the Tweed-Faced Boy. (He was still tickling Brian because they were both enjoying it and because he had realized that there wasn't a damsel inside him.) The Tweed-Faced Boy looked around the kitchen and speared a rather dusty pancake with his pretend sword. "And I have to follow those eyes and that mouth before they disappear! Farewell!" He jumped out of the kitchen window, leaving muddy footprints on the sill.

"Oh, Uncle Shawn!" said Bill. And because Bill was cross and had been hypnotized, he then said a terrible thing: "This is ALL YOUR FAULT!"

Uncle Shawn looked at Bill with his clever, big blue eyes and he didn't say anything. Which was part of his plan.

"Maybe Doctor P'Klawz is right and you are too Unusual." Bill had a nasty wriggly feeling in his tummy when he said this.

Uncle Shawn nodded and ruffled his hair so that it nodded, too. "Well... Maybe I am an Unusual person." He smiled a small, sad smile. "Maybe I should go and be squished in the Institution for Maximum Security and Unusualness Curing."

This made Bill stop being angry altogether, because thinking of Uncle Shawn – who was filled up to the top with fun – being left alone with P'Klawz was horrible. "No, no... That might be not a good idea..." Bill knew that without his Unusualness, Uncle Shawn wouldn't be Uncle Shawn anymore...

NASTY WRIGGLY FEELING

But Uncle Shawn seemed very happy about going to the Institution. "Oh, I think it will be wonderful! That will solve all our problems. I should go at once."

Everyone in the room – especially Bill – thought that sounded terrible.

"I will stay until I am Usual!" Uncle Shawn grinned.

Everyone shivered all over until their fur was standing on end and they looked as if they'd been washed and then rubbed with towels.

But Uncle Shawn just winked at Bill and said, "I'll go right away. Goodness me, it's almost as if things are running exactly according to some kind of plan. Why don't you phone Doctor P'Klawz for me? Here's his card." And then Uncle Shawn walked out, whistling as if there was nothing worrying him at all. 🐾

SECTION TWELVE

In which we have the saddest section in the history of sections. But maybe Uncle Shawn has a plan. I do hope so. I really do. Otherwise...

Badger Bill looked at his friends the llamas and then he looked at P'Klawz's card. His tummy flip-flopped.

Guinevere said, "But an Institution for Maximum Security and Unusualness Curing sounds horrible."

And Carlos said, "I don't think they would let us visit him there."

And Ginalolobrigida said, "I am wonderful

and charming. I would be allowed to visit."

Bill said, in a sad and trembly voice, "Uncle Shawn did tell me to phone Dr. P'Klawz... And I suppose..."

"Don't send him away," said Brian. "I'll be scared if he goes away." Brian swallowed loudly. "He might be scared, too..."

The other llamas nodded. Carlos sniffled.

And Bill thought of how much he would miss Uncle Shawn.

But then Bill thought about the whole house being full of dust and hoofprints and llama fur, and the floating eyes and mouth, and the boy with a tweed mask and a pirate hat – and what about the big eyes and the big voice in the sea...?

Bill felt so confused his ears lay flat against his head and stopped moving.

Because he trusted Uncle Shawn, his best friend, he did what he had been told to do – even though it made him feel sick. He went and phoned Dr.

P'Klawz and everybody heard him say, "Hello? Doctor P'Klawz? Uncle Shawn wants you to take him away and make him less Unusual."

BILL'S MOODS: A POCKET GUIDE

HAPPY
BOUNCY EARS
EYES LOOKING FORWARD TO CHRISTMAS
COMFY NOSE FUR
JOLLY TOES

SAD
LIFELESS EARS
EYES DOWN
SLOPING SHOULDERS
FLAT NOSE FUR
MISERABLE TOES

Oh dear!

The llamas went out and waited at the front of the farmhouse and were very quiet and leaned against each other and rubbed noses so that they wouldn't feel so worried. Ginalolobrigida even kissed the top of Brian's head so that he would be less upset. And Guinevere cried a bit and Carlos said, "It's OK. Please don't cry. Maybe Uncle Shawn has a plan." Only he didn't sound as if he believed that.

After a while, a huge gray van arrived. On the side of the van there were some nasty big words: **INSTITUTION FOR MAXIMUM SECURITY AND UNUSUALNESS CURING – COLLECTION SERVICE.**

Uncle Shawn came out and waved at the van as if it was full of delicious ice cream.

Two huge gray men in huge gray coats climbed out of the van and stood silently with their arms folded.

Brian Llama looked at them and said, "Oh

HUGE GRAY VAN

HUGE GRAY COATS

no," very quietly.

Dr. P'Klawz stepped out of the back of the van, wearing his shiny shoes and his perfectly white suit, and grinned like a thousand toilets covered by a big horrible snowdrift. And he said in an evil and pleased voice, "I told you that your friends would want to get rid of you, Uncle Shawn." He waved the piece of paper Bill had refused to sign, even while he was hypnotized. P'Klawz had forged Bill's signature on it. "Here is proof that your best friend doesn't like you." He

CRUEL ICEBERG

YOU LOOK SILLY IN THAT HAT

grinned like a cruel iceberg. "Come along now – or you'll be late for your first meal of gray porridge and hot water."

Brian whispered, "But Uncle Shawn won't like that. He'd prefer fish and chips, or custard and chops, or chocolate sausages."

The other llamas nodded, too nervous to speak, but P'Klawz ignored them. He twirled his shiny watch and it made them all feel a bit sleepy.

Then Bill opened the front door. He was so sad all his fur had gone droopy and he could hardly lift his head. He was carrying a small bag with nice things that Uncle Shawn might like to take with him. Uncle Shawn waved at him and said, "Thank you, Bill. You're still my best friend. And you know what best friends do."

"No waving. No friends," said P'Klawz. "And no bags. Every inmate wears a gray smock. We will give you the smock. That's all you need."

"Oh, well then," said Uncle Shawn. "That will be fine." Uncle Shawn shook Bill's paw very seriously and said, "Do not worry, very dear Bill. You are my best friend in the whole world and everything will be fine from now on." And he winked an enormous wink – as if he really did have a plan. Or most of a plan. Bill didn't notice, though, because he was upset and staring at the ground and thinking that he might cry.

Uncle Shawn walked towards Dr. P'Klawz and called out to the llamas, "Take care of each other while I am away, dear Carlos and Guinevere and Ginalolobrigida and – of course – dear Brian. You must come and visit me soon." He sounded cheery but Uncle Shawn's hair looked very still and worried.

"No visitors!" said P'Klawz firmly.

"Maybe a postcard or two…"

"No postcards! Come along. You are wasting time." And P'Klawz pushed Uncle Shawn into the van, before climbing in and shutting the doors behind him with a big gray THUMP.

The two men in gray got into the front of the van. Then the van drove away, and Bill and the llamas watched Uncle Shawn's face get smaller and smaller as the van's tiny rear window went farther and farther into the distance.

In the end, they couldn't see Uncle Shawn, or even the van.

And then they all sat down together on the grass, because they were too sad to go anywhere else, and pretended they weren't crying.

But they all were.

And Bill was crying most of all.

DEFINITELY NOT CRYING

The day after that – which was a Tuesday – Guinevere and Carlos tried to have a fight about who had the biggest bottom, but they were too sad to argue.

Carlos said to an especially tall flower, "Oh, Juan... I miss Uncle Shawn."

Guinevere tried to say, "That's not Juan, you silly llama." But in the end, all the words got mixed up and came out sounding like, "I miss Uncle Shawn, too."

They both went and drank some lemonade in one of the llama barns, but it tasted too salty because Badger Bill had been crying while he made it.

On Wednesday, Brian Llama woke up at two in the morning and was sure he heard something like tiny footsteps and sighing. He considered yelling and running away, but he felt too tired and upset. He just lay on top of his bed made of straw and said, "Oh, I miss Uncle Shawn."

"I probably do, too," said the dark. And then it sighed. It was Linvizzygirl, of course.

Brian Llama felt someone the shape and size of

LINVIZZYGIRL

a little girl leaning against his side and using his fur as a pillow. Somehow he didn't mind, because the voice sounded almost as sad as he was.

On Thursday, Ginalolobrigida Llama was

A LITTLE POOL

trying to admire her reflection in a little pool near the edge of the woods. She knew she had the most glimmering eyes and the most seductive long nose of any llama anywhere. But today she thought that her nose seemed squint and one of her eyelashes seemed to be shorter than the rest.

She suddenly realized, "Being terribly sad is ruining my beauty. If I go on missing Uncle Shawn,

I shall look like the most hideous witch in the world." (As you know, the most hideous witch in the world is Carmilla Newtfeet. She is so ugly that even writing down her name can turn your teeth green.)

GINALOLOBRIGIDA, LLAMA

FABULOUS EYES

ROMANTICALLY WAVING HAIR

SMELLS OF VIOLETS AND BEAUTY

LUSH LASHES

CARMILLA NEWTFEET, WITCH

TERRIFYING HAIR

EVIL STARING EYES

SMELLS OF 100-YEAR-OLD CHEESE AND OTHER PEOPLE'S TEARS

CLAMMY FEET

Ginalolobrigida sighed and dipped one of her beautifully varnished hooves into the pool so that her reflection went wibbly.

"Perfect and lovely damsel, may I assist thee?" shouted a voice.

122

Ginalolobrigida looked up to see the Tweed-Faced Boy sitting in a tree above her.

"I am not a damsel, I am a llama."

"Everyone says that."

"Everyone who is a llama will always say that. Why do you have a tweed mask? Did you get so sad you became ugly?"

The Tweed-Faced Boy scratched under his newspaper hat while he thought. "I don't think so – it's more that I need to be in disguise. You see, Doctor P'Klawz hypnotized my mother so that she would let him take me away to be squished. He had already taken my sister. He kept me and a few others in a small Institution, far away from here, and fed us gray porridge and made us sew pillowcases that would give people nightmares. I looked for my sister there but she must have been somewhere else... When P'Klawz moved all of us to the new Institution here, I escaped and started wearing this mask so

123

that no one would find me and take me back."

"I see," said Ginalolobrigida, even though she didn't really.

"I have sworn to defend all damsels in distress until I find my sister and save her. You haven't seen a little girl around here, have you? She'd be about my height. We're twins. She was born a few minutes before me, but I'm a bit bigger and so I have to look after her. At least, I'm supposed to. I don't know the way back home, or how to rescue her, or anything... But I must have my revenge on P'Klawz!"

"Does she have a face?" asked Ginalolobrigida, thinking of Linvizzygirl.

"Of course she has a face! And it was nice and... I miss her." The Tweed-Faced Boy's head drooped.

"No, I haven't seen any little girl's faces around here. And I don't know if you can defeat P'Klawz using a pretend sword," said Ginalolobrigida.

TWEED-FACED BOY IN TREE

LLAMA IN DISTRESS

The Tweed-Faced Boy nodded sadly. "I know. I'm not big enough to be much use yet." Then he cheered up a bit – he was a brave young person. "Are you a llama in distress? Should I defend you?"

"I am in distress, but that is because I am missing my friend, Uncle Shawn. He has been taken away."

Tweed-Faced Boy looked at her sharply and

said, "Did you send him to the Institution?"

"We didn't want to…"

Ginalolobrigida was about to explain that Uncle Shawn had asked to go when the boy started to shout, "People and llamas who send their friends to P'Klawz are horrible! I'm going to keep on looking for my sister. We care about each other – the way you should care about your friend." And he climbed higher and higher into his tree, and soon was climbing into another and another, getting farther away.

"Oh dear," sighed Ginalolobrigida. "I'm too sad to even brush my fur."

And she knew that the Tweed-Faced Boy was right. They had made a terrible mistake when they sent Uncle Shawn away.

BOILED ICE CREAM

SECTION THIRTEEN

In which there is a little bit of sadness and some very bad baking. And Badger Bill has an idea. It is a very good idea indeed. Hooray!

On Friday, Badger Bill got out of bed after not really sleeping. He went downstairs to find the house neat and tidy and empty. All the llamas had helped him to clean it and now they were too scared to come inside in case they made a mess.

Badger Bill didn't go outside because he felt guilty for having phoned Dr. P'Klawz, even though Uncle Shawn had asked him to. And not one of his friends was there to give him a hug.

Badger Bill had cooked and baked lots and lots of food on Tuesday, Wednesday and Thursday, just to keep himself busy. Everything he cooked turned out sadly, though. He burned the toast. He boiled the ice cream. He fried the chocolate. And big, slow badger tears rolled down his big stripy nose and made everything taste salty.

"Oh, Uncle Shawn..." sighed Badger Bill. He went and sat in Uncle Shawn's armchair and thought, "What would you do now?"

But he couldn't think of anything.

His ears flopped miserably.

But then – he thought.

And then – he smiled.

And then – he knew!

"Uncle Shawn smiled when he went away. Uncle Shawn only smiles when he's happy. And he winked at me. And he said the word PLAN." Bill stood up and danced a little dance and his ears started to look like badger ears again.

"UNCLE SHAWN HAS A PLAN!!!!"

Bill jumped and nearly hit his head on the ceiling he was so excited. "Or maybe ... HE WANTS US TO HAVE A PLAN!" Bill thought of all history's clever badgers and he stood up very straight and

HISTORY'S CLEVER BADGERS

PERCY BADGER

PHYSICIST WHO RAN INTO APPLE TREE WITH HIS SCOOTER, CAUSING APPLE TO FALL ON ISAAC NEWTON.

EMILY BADGER

INVENTOR OF THE SILENT TROMBONE FOR SHY PEOPLE.

MARGARET BADGER

INVENTED SHOELACES. AND THEN INVENTED SHOES.

WILBERFORCE BADGER

DISCOVERED MAMMOTHS WENT EXTINCT BECAUSE THEY BECAME IRRELEFANT.

really believed that he could rescue his best friend, if he tried hard enough. "I will make a plan." Maybe he could get a bit of help from his friends, too. "YES! We'll make a plan! All of us together!"

He ran outside as fast as his short-but-handsome legs would take him and yelled, "EVERYONE!!! WE NEED A PLAN!!!"

Up in the corner of the ceiling in the farmhouse living room, a large and friendly spider called Claude bounced up and down on a length of spider silk and was very excited about what Bill and everyone else might plan. He also thought, "I wonder what Uncle Shawn has been doing all this time?" 🐾

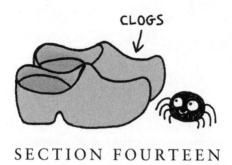
CLOGS

SECTION FOURTEEN

In which – here is Uncle Shawn! This section contains smocks. And clogs. And dancing. This would please Claude the spider because he has lots of legs for dancing.

Uncle Shawn had been doing a lot.

All the llamas and especially Bill had looked miserable from their feet right up to their ears as he left on Monday, but Uncle Shawn couldn't say, "Don't worry! I have a plan!" P'Klawz couldn't even suspect there might be a plan. Uncle Shawn needed to get all the way inside the Institution to see what was going on, so he

UNCLE SHAWN

INSTITUTION FOR MAXIMUM SECURITY AND UNUSUALNESS CURING COLLECTION SERVICE

had to let everything seem sad for a little while. Inside the gray van, he thought, "My plan isn't exactly finished and maybe someone going behind locked gates and locked doors and a high fence should have all of a plan – especially if he will also be dealing with guards and a terrible man who hates happiness. But I'm sure that everything will work out well... Or almost sure, anyway."

While the van drove to the Institution for Maximum Security and Unusualness Curing – which was beyond the village and behind the Droochit Hills – Dr. P'Klawz tried to make Uncle Shawn miserable. "There will be nothing but gray porridge and a gray smock for you." He

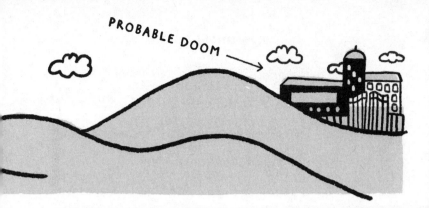

PROBABLE DOOM →

tried grinning, but his grin was a bit small – like a little evil mixing bowl.

Uncle Shawn crossed his long legs out in front of him and stretched, as if he was enjoying the ride. He hummed a little tune to himself.

"Stop humming!"

"I can't help it," Uncle Shawn said. "I always hum when I'm having a lovely time."

"You're not meant to be having a lovely time! You're meant to be heartbroken and lonely and scared!"

"Oh, but that wouldn't be any fun at all," said Uncle Shawn. And then he leaned in close to P'Klawz and whispered, "You could do better than this and be much nicer. And you have until we reach the Institution to decide whether you will. After that, it will be too late." And his very blue eyes looked right through P'Klawz and out the other side and made him shiver.

P'Klawz shook his head and said, "No, Uncle Shawn. It is too late for you. Soon I will have squished the happiest man in Scotland and I will take your farm from your stupid talking animals and build a new Institution on top of it! And I will keep building Institutions until there is no fun or happiness anywhere!"

"Oh dear." Uncle Shawn frowned.

"Now you're worried! Ha!" shouted P'Klawz.

"No," said Uncle Shawn. "I am sorry. That is a very great shame for you."

And then Uncle Shawn stared at P'Klawz's hair that looked as if it had been painted on *because it was painted on*. It was just Hair In A Tin – as sold to gentlemen with reduced head foliage everywhere.

HAIR IN A TIN

AS SOLD TO GENTLEMEN WITH REDUCED HEAD FOLIAGE EVERYWHERE

NO ONE WILL EVER KNOW!

Patented Perfect HAIR PAINT

10g

DON'T GIVE IN! GET HAIR IN A TIN!

IN THREE LIFELIKE COLORS!

Uncle Shawn stared harder until P'Klawz could feel himself blushing. And then Uncle Shawn winked a very large wink aimed at the top of P'Klawz's head and closed his eyes as if he felt like a comfy snooze.

135

After that, P'Klawz couldn't grin even a tiny bit.

On Tuesday, Uncle Shawn woke up in one of the big, long dormitories of the Institution and discovered that all his clothes had been taken away and replaced with a gray inmate smock that didn't fit very well and wasn't very warm.

When Uncle Shawn put on the smock, he

thought it looked so silly and felt so flippy-floppy and baggy that it made him giggle. And the wooden inmate clogs he had to wear on his feet were so clacketty that he couldn't help dancing. This also helped him to get warm in the chilly room.

The other inmates looked at him while he danced and were very puzzled. Some of them had been in P'Klawz's Institutions for so long, they had forgotten what fun looked like.

They watched as Uncle Shawn clacketty-clicketty danced along the corridor and then they listened while he sang in the cold shower and made *brrrrr* noises as he dried himself with the thin gray inmate towel, then came back and announced, "That's the most wonderful shower I have ever had!"

One of the guards said, "Don't you worry – the gray porridge will soon change how cheerful you are."

But when Uncle Shawn danced into the long, gray dining hall – *clacketty, clicketty, clocketty* – and collected his porridge, he looked even happier. He sat down on one of the dining benches between a small child inmate and a grown-up he recognized as once having been the owner of the Pandrumdroochit ice cream shop. Uncle Shawn winked at them both and announced, "Mmmmm! Lovely! This is the grayest porridge I have ever seen!" Then he ate it quickly, as if it was delicious. All the inmates stared at him. But, tucked away in a corner, inmate number 424 (who was really Hughie who liked to play at being a spaceman) smiled a tiny secret smile. Uncle Shawn's clever blue eyes spotted this and one of them winked at Hughie.

The gray guards also stared at Uncle Shawn. He definitely seemed to be having fun.

When Uncle Shawn joined the inmates at work printing leaflets about Unusualness, he added drawings of smiley faces and hearts and wrote jokes on the back.

The gray guards noticed this and moved Uncle Shawn to the department where inmates folded the washed smocks. But Uncle Shawn folded his smocks into the shapes of mountains and elephants and swans. And he danced while he did it.

UNCLE SHAWN'S SMOCKORIGAMI!

WHY NOT FOLD YOUR REGULATION GRAY SMOCK INTO ONE OF THESE FUN SHAPES?

MOUNTAINS

ELEPHANT

ANGRY BADGER

VERY UNUSUAL UNCLE

EVIL PRETEND DOCTOR

So the gray guards put Uncle Shawn outside in the cold to sweep the hard concrete exercise yard. Only this made Uncle Shawn dance his special clog dance even harder and faster, and practice new bits of leaping and twirling so that he got very good at it and kept very warm. And all over the Institution, the inmates could hear him.

Swoosh – click – swoosh – clack – swoosh – spin – swoosh – hop – swoosh – leap.

He sounded Unusually Happy.

On Wednesday, when all the inmates were sent outside to the exercise yard, Uncle Shawn danced in his clogs and smock for the whole of exercise time and several inmates (including Hughie) actually giggled and tapped their feet.

And then two and then four and then lots of inmates decided they would try dancing in the exercise yard themselves, and this made them feel warmer and more like the people they had been. As the big gray yard began to clitter and clatter

and clutter and clooter with clogs, the gray guards felt strange and some of them went indoors and had to sit down and have cups of tea and phone their mums.

During dinner, some inmates started humming as if they were happy. And Hughie (who had never forgotten being a spaceman) gobbled his porridge as if it was especially delicious and announced, "My, this is wonderful porridge! It tastes as if it has honey and raspberries in it!"

The others looked at him and then inmate 223, who was really called Hani, shouted, "Mine tastes of sunshine and toffee!" This made some of the inmates laugh. And inmate Angus said quietly, "My porridge tastes just the way it did at home with my children." And another inmate, called Mary, said, "My porridge tastes how it did when my husband made it on Sundays." And slowly each one of the inmates started talking about their porridge, but really they were talking about who they used to be and the things they used to like.

The gray guards watched all this happening and didn't know what to do. They tried yelling but nobody paid any attention. Some inmates even went back and asked for more porridge and the Institution porridge cooks let them have it, because no one had ever appreciated their porridge before (it was quite disgusting), and they suddenly felt happy, too. One of them, called Doreen, thought about actually cooking the porridge with milk tomorrow and putting some bananas on top, because then people would like it even more and be even nicer to her.

All this made the gray guards very worried.

They left the inmates alone with Uncle Shawn and went up to Dr. P'Klawz's office, high in the gray tower that watched over the whole Institution for Maximum Security and Unusualness Curing.

P'Klawz was hiding under his desk.

"Why are you hiding under your desk?" asked the biggest of the gray guards, who was called Henry Witherbottom.

FRAMED PHOTO OF HIMSELF

SPIDER SWATTER

INMATE PHOTOS

LIBRARY BOOK HE HASN'T RETURNED

SHIN OINTMENT

"Go away," whispered P'Klawz. "My shins have gone flaky and my hair hurts."

(Because P'Klawz was so wicked, all his real hair had left him when he was twelve and gone to be extra chest hair for a rock star called Simon Diamante. That's why P'Klawz had to paint his head.)

SIMON DIAMANTE

WORLD'S MANLIEST ROCK STAR FOR 18th YEAR*
*may contain some goat hair

Henry Witherbottom thought this sounded a bit Unusual. "Can we help you with anything, sir?"

"People are being happy. I can feel it. There is fun breaking out. Stop it at once!"

"But how, sir?" asked Henry. "Uncle Shawn is happy all the time. He doesn't even have an inmate number because he distracted the guard who gives out the numbers by talking to him

144

about the sound dogs' paws make. We have to just call him Uncle Shawn..."

"Stop bothering me! Just go and do what I told you!" yelled P'Klawz and he curled up in a ball and wouldn't say anything else.

The gray guards all tiptoed away in their big creaky boots.

When the gray guards got down to the dining hall, Uncle Shawn and the inmates had finished all the porridge and *were dancing*. They were all clacketty-clicketty-clocketty-clucketty dancing in their clogs and waving their baggy smocks about and swooshing their arms and bowing to each other. And *they were smiling*.

The gray guards were amazed. Some of them smiled, too, because the dancing was so happy and funny and silly. A small guard called Peter even found that he was bobbing up and down and swaying to the rhythm.

Uncle Shawn grinned and called to them,

"Hello, guards! We're dancing the Clog and Smock Dance. It's great fun. Come and join us."

Henry was puzzled. "Your smocks are ugly and they don't fit and they're the dullest color in the world, and your clogs are all clacketty and hard to walk in. How can you be having fun?"

"Why, because we have decided to have fun in spite of them. And the more fun we have, the warmer we get and the more we forget our numbers and remember our names. We don't have to be inmates – we can be lots of other things. We can be people who are kind to each other and happy. We could even be not inside this Institution."

Henry chewed the end of his shirt collar – he had always done this when he was nervous, even at school. He told his guards to surround the dancers and look sternly at them.

The gray guards tried.

But quite a few of them started to giggle and clap in time to the dancing.

THE CLOG AND SMOCK DANCE

SLIDE

PIROUETTE

KICK ×5

JUMP ×2

Upstairs, P'Klawz's aches got a lot worse, because suddenly there was even more fun in the Institution for Maximum Security and Unusualness Curing.

On Thursday morning, there were bits of banana on top of everyone's sweet, milky porridge. Everyone thought this was wonderful and cheered and shook porridge cook Doreen's hand. By lunchtime, another porridge cook, called Colin, had found some honey and the inmates were so delighted to have honey on their porridge that there was dancing for most of the afternoon and no work. (The gray guards were too slow to

THINGS THAT MAKE HORRIBLE PORRIDGE NICER

1. HONEY

2. BANANAS

3. HAPPY MEMORIES

148

catch the dancers and didn't know whether they should, because P'Klawz couldn't give them any orders – his teeth hurt too much.) The clacketty-clicketty-clocketty-clucketty-clooketty noise of the clogs shook the loose, drafty windows of the Institution until they rattled cheerfully.

On Thursday evening, everyone was eating their honey-and-banana porridge and thinking about new dances. Some of the gray guards were sitting on the floor and reading letters from home, because it was less tiring than standing up and looking menacing. But then, in the middle of all the happy chatting and laughter and joke telling, Dr. P'Klawz suddenly appeared in the dining hall.

He could hardly control his teeth, which sounded like all the brakes on an express train. "SILENCE – *SKREE!*" he shouted. The guards stood up and pulled their gray uniforms straight and buttoned their collars. The inmates went quiet and remembered being miserable.

P'Klawz had a towel wrapped around his head to try and keep the happiness out. It was making his head hot and sweaty so that his painted hair was starting to drip into his eyes. It was also running down his neck and ruining his perfectly white collar. "ENOUGH!" he screamed. And he took out his hypnotizing watch and twirled it. "Go to your dormitories! The gray guards will lock you in and you will not get any breakfast or lunch or dinner tomorrow!"

This nearly made Henry the guard say, "That's a bit nasty." But then he caught sight of the watch and kept quiet instead.

"You will have all of tomorrow to think about how Unusual you have been! And remember, this is all Uncle Shawn's fault. He is the one who insisted on making you happy!"

Uncle Shawn could hear some of the small child inmates crying and he didn't like that. Inside he was angry.

TOWEL WRAPPED AROUND HEAD TO TRY AND KEEP THE HAPPINESS OUT

SWEATY HEAD

PAINTED HAIR DRIPPING

RUINING HIS PERFECTLY WHITE COLLAR

And he was even more angry as everyone was marched back to their dormitories and the big locks on the doors were turned with horrible clunks.

While he told the inmates in his dormitory jokes and funny stories to stop them being too sad, Uncle Shawn stayed angry.

It is never a good or a wise thing to make Uncle Shawn angry...

And Uncle Shawn thought, "This all needs to change. I wonder if Bill and the llamas have a plan? Their plan and my plan could join up to make one big gargantunormous plan... That's what we need." He smiled and the cold, dark air that chilled the bed frames got a bit warmer. "They are wonderful llamas and a wonderful badger – I think they will have a very fine plan..." 🐾

SECTION FIFTEEN

In which there are lots of ears and legs,

and a gargantunormous plan that might

get Uncle Shawn and all the inmates out of

the Institution... At least we hope so.

The next day, while Uncle Shawn and the orphans tried to keep happy by dancing in their dormitories – even though they were getting hungrier and hungrier – Badger Bill and the llamas were trying to make plans.

Only they weren't exactly good at plans.

Bill had put a big piece of paper on the kitchen table (which wasn't a llama under a quilt) and then he had written: **PLAN TO RESCUE UNCLE SHAWN.**

After that, things had gotten a bit difficult.

And Claude the spider was wondering how to say he'd like to help, because spiders don't really speak. So he just bounced on his silk – like a yo-yo with lots of legs.

Brian Llama said, "The Institution has big, high fences and tall iron gates and searchlights and everything."

"Well, then let's dig a tunnel," said Bill. Badgers are good at tunnels.

"That sounds very dusty and dirty," said Ginalolobrigida.

"I know!" said Guinevere. "We could get a helicopter and fly over the walls, and we could jump out wearing dark pullovers and hats and then rescue everyone."

Bill put his paws over his ears in frustration. "We don't know how to fly a helicopter – and we

154

PLAN TO RESCUE UNCLE SHAWN

1. 2. FLY OVER THE WALLS IN A HELICOPTER.
3. JUMP OUT WEARING DARK PULLOVERS.
DIG A TUNNEL.
4. RESCUE EVERYONE.

don't have one! We don't even have pullovers and … and … poor Uncle Shawn is in that nasty place and IT'S HORRIBLE AND I MISS HIM."

After that, Bill and the llamas just sat and felt sad and lonely.

And then a voice that didn't seem to belong to anyone said, "I'm hungry." And a scone lifted off the scone dish, floated in midair and was slowly eaten by an invisible mouth.

Bill and Carlos and Guinivere were very scared by this, and yelled, "*EMERGENCIA!*" But Ginalolobrigida just said to a patch of air, "Oh,

155

you've taken off your makeup. A lady is invisible without the proper makeup."

Brian – which surprised everyone – wasn't scared even a bit. He just said, "That's who tickles my ears and strokes my nose when I'm scared at night. She keeps the swamp monsters and the giant hungry owls away. She leans her head against my tummy where the fur is very soft and takes naps."

"Good heavens," said everyone except Ginalolobrigida, who explained, "This is a young invisible human girl called Linvizzygirl."

Just then there was a loud thumping at the door.

"*Aaahhh! Emergencia!*" said Brian. "They've come back to take us away for being Unusual!"

But when Bill went and opened the door with shaking paws, there stood the Tweed-Faced Boy.

"I heard cries for help! I will rescue you!"

Bill sighed. "It's not us who needs rescuing – it's Uncle Shawn."

THINGS THAT SCARE BRIAN LLAMA AT NIGHT

1. SWAMP MONSTERS

2. GIANT HUNGRY OWLS

3. GHOSTS

THINGS THAT DON'T SCARE HIM

1. YOUNG INVISIBLE HUMAN GIRLS

"Is he a damsel?"

"He's an uncle."

Bill took the Tweed-Faced Boy back to the kitchen, where Linvizzygirl had eaten another two scones and an apple.

"He's been taken by Doctor P'Klawz," explained Bill.

"Yes, and that's not something that should happen to anyone," said the Tweed-Faced Boy, looking a bit smaller and worried but also cross. "I've been an inmate in one of his Institutions and they're terrible. Anything to do with P'Klawz is always terrible. I have sworn my revenge on him. And you should never have let your friend go and see him, not even for a visit, never mind letting P'Klawz lock him away." He shook his sword, but the shoelace came loose and it turned back into two sticks.

"If you managed to get away from an Institution... Could you manage to get into one?" asked Bill, his ears at an excited angle.

EARS AT AN EXCITED ANGLE

"It would be very hard..." The Tweed-Faced Boy scratched his newspaper hat sadly.

By now, Claude was so enthusiastic that he quickly spelled out, in spider silk:

Let us help too, please.

He was a very polite spider.

Bill noticed the spider writing and said, "Hello?"

Claude bounced down on his thread and smiled as much as spiders can – which isn't much. (This made Brian squeal.) And then Claude wrote out – quite slowly:

**The World
Association of Spiders
(Pandrumdroochit Branch)
will help you.**

Because P'Klawz drove spiders from all the corners of all his rooms and squashed them whenever he could, spiders everywhere did not like him.

Everyone tried to be pleased about Claude's offer of help, but also felt a bit shivery, because spiders can seem scary.

"I like spiders, though," said Carlos.

"All right, then," said Bill. "Let's make a plan. Claude – you can write it down in spiderweb."

Linvizzygirl tickled Brian's ears and made him grin and then everyone made a wonderful plan together. Or most of one. 🐾

TIRED AND HUNGRY

SECTION SIXTEEN

In which there is a lunchtime with no lunch in it, which is always very sad. There are some googly eyes and some rudeness. And there is some Lovely Unusualness! Uncle Shawn's plan is beginning to work...

By lunchtime at the Institution for Maximum Security and Unusualness Curing, Uncle Shawn and the inmates were really hungry. Dancing had kept them warm, but it had used up lots of their strength. Hani and Angus and Hughie and the other inmates were flopped on the floor in a heap because they were so tired.

161

"Not long now," Uncle Shawn told them. "Soon my plan will meet in the middle with my friends' plan and then... Everything will be wonderful. Or really scary. Or both."

Doctor P'Klawz had ordered the gray guards to turn off even the tiny bit of heating that kept the insides of the windows from freezing up. The room was now so cold that you could see your breath in big, miserable clouds.

Uncle Shawn said, "If it's so cold, let's make a pretend igloo."

So the inmates piled up the thin, mean mattresses and made them into one big warm platform they could sit on, and then they huddled up together under the blankets in their make-believe igloo.

Then Uncle Shawn said, "You are all here for being Unusual, aren't you?"

The inmates nodded their heads as if this was terrible news.

Uncle Shawn's blue eyes sparkled. "Then you

BIG, MISERABLE CLOUD

MAKE-BELIEVE IGLOO

must be very good at being Unusual. Why don't you try some Unusualness to keep you warm?"

"It's been too long since we did anything but copy out leaflets and eat gray porridge and do what we're told," said a very small, tired inmate called Kemal.

"Well then allow me to demonstrate," said Uncle Shawn. And even though he was tired and cold and hungry, he ruffled up his hair so that it wriggled and jiggled in an Unusual way.

He clucked like a chicken and made a face like a goat and made his big blue eyes go googly. The inmates started to giggle. Then he sang in an Unusual voice, "*Oooh-HUHOO-boiOIOIng*," and wibbled his knees.

Soon all the inmates were laughing and hooting and singing their own silly songs.

"*Yoogah yoogah yoogah. SPLAH!*"

And also:

"*We hate P'Klawz*

And the locks on his doors.

His hair is fake

Like the icing on a cake!"

Hughie got up and walked like a spaceman and made spaceman sounds: "*Skshshshsh… Woopwoopwoop.*" And he described a spaceman exploring while the inmates cheered. "I am exploring… I am exploring… *Skshshshsh…* And I have discovered … Doctor P'Klawz has a silly bottom!"

The walls and floors of the Institution were so

164

DOCTOR P'KLAWZ HAS A SILLY BOTTOM!

flimsy that all of the other inmates locked in their dormitories could hear people being rude about P'Klawz and having fun, so they started to join in.

Uncle Shawn held competitions to see who was best at not laughing. Pairs of inmates stared and stared and stared at each other until it was impossible not to giggle. (You can try this game yourself. Even if you look at your own face in a mirror, after a while, you will find that your

Unusualness will make you laugh.)

Upstairs in his office, Dr. P'Klawz now had two towels wrapped around his head. His shins were itching, so he had taken off his socks and rolled up his trousers. This meant that Henry Witherbottom, the guard, had to look at P'Klawz's bony white ankles and hairy white shins.

"Can I get you a nice cup of tea?" asked Henry, who was trying not to snigger at P'Klawz's shins.

"Just make it stop! The whole building is full of Unusual happiness and happy Unusualness! It is making my teeth rattle." Doctor P'Klawz's teeth did look like bits of very angry bathtub, and sounded like a train being sandpapered. "*SKREEEE-eeeee-EEEEE.* Go and dig a big hole in the Institution grounds and then make Uncle Shawn stand in it and put a lid over the top. Don't let him out until he stops being Unusual and happy!"

"Oh no…" said Henry. "That would be horrible."

"Then tie him up with rope until only his nose is showing and he can't dance!" yelled P'Klawz. He tried twirling his shiny watch, but his hands were shaking so much that it just wobbled.

PAINT SPLATTERS

STREAKY HAIR DRIPS

HAIRY WHITE SHINS

BONY WHITE ANKLES

Henry folded his arms and said, "That's even worse. And anyway, we used up all the rope in the guards' jump rope competition..." He said the last bit quietly because the guards hadn't asked permission to jump rope. But Henry was remembering how much he liked fun.

"Idiot!" shouted P'Klawz and he was about to be even more rude to Henry when the bell sounded from the Institution gates.

167

"Shall I go and see who that is?" asked Henry.

"No! I will go," said P'Klawz, pulling the towels from around his head, even though this made his brain hurt a lot more. (It also revealed that his Hair In A Tin had almost completely gone. The top of his head looked like a streaky, dirty egg.) "Tell all the guards to shout at the inmates and remove their blankets."

Henry thought this was a really nasty idea. And, with the Institution filling up with happiness and Unusualness, he decided he might forget all about it...

P'Klawz straightened his white suit – which was spattered with Hair In A Tin – and made his face look as trustworthy and kind as possible. His teeth kept on grinding and rattling and grating – *skreeeee-reee-EEEE-eeee* – while he tried to smile. This looked so horrible that bits of paint fell off the walls as he passed by.

And – oh goodness me, no! – as P'Klawz walked

through the Institution, he spoke to his two favorite guards who were called 5557 and 5555, because they thought names were Too Unusual and they preferred numbers. They liked P'Klawz's nastiness, because it made their own nastiness even nastier.

GRUMPY HAIR

UNUSUALLY STUPID AND NASTY THOUGHTS

UNUSUALLY NASTY THOUGHTS

ANGRY NOSE HAIR

SUSPICIOUS FROWN

INMATE SLAPPING HAND

GROWLY TEETH

INMATE KICKING BOOTS

INMATE PINCHING FINGERS

GUARD 5557

GUARD 5555

P'Klawz told 5557 and 5555 to go and take Uncle Shawn to the Squishing Room in the basement!

And once he was there ... *they should squish him at once until all his Unusualness was gone!!!*

Oh no! What will we do now? *EMERGENCIA!!!!!*

VERY, VERY SCARED

SHAKING KNEES →

SECTION SEVENTEEN

In which while we are worrying about Uncle Shawn, there is an unexpected big bottom and an excellent disguise. Brian Llama is Unusually Brave. And a cloud appears – an Unusual cloud. Badger Bill's plan is beginning to work...

When Dr. P'Klawz reached the Institution gates, he saw a perfectly normal grown-up standing beside a small boy wearing a tweed mask. That was just the kind of Unusualness that should be handed over to his Institution. P'Klawz smiled like a white tiger hiding in rice pudding.

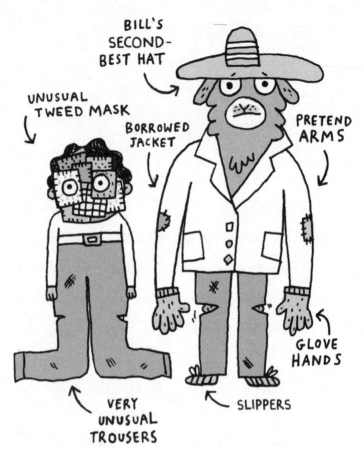

BILL'S SECOND-BEST HAT

UNUSUAL TWEED MASK

BORROWED JACKET

PRETEND ARMS

GLOVE HANDS

VERY UNUSUAL TROUSERS

SLIPPERS

In fact, the two people at the gate were the Tweed-Faced Boy and Brian Llama. Brian was terrified and his knees were shaking – but they were hidden inside trousers just now, because he was *in disguise*.

172

Brian did not look like Brian at all. Ginalolobrigida – an expert in all beauty techniques – had plaited Brian's long and thick llama fur into big pigtails. These were shoved inside the sleeves of one of Uncle Shawn's jackets to look like arms and had gloves attached to look like hands – especially if you had a terrible headache, which P'Klawz did. Brian was also wearing a wide hat he'd borrowed from Bill and he had put Uncle Shawn's trousers on his front legs. As long as you only looked at him from the front, he seemed to be a human person with thin, wibbly arms and a very long nose.

"Yes, may I help you? *Skreeee* – I beg your pardon. I mean, I am the famous Doctor P' – *skree* – Klawz."

Brian was an expert in all kinds of being worried, so he was very convincing when he said, "Ah, Doctor Pickles. I am really, really worried!"

"P'Klawz!"

"Bless you. I am sooo worried. I am … um

... Mr. Smith and this small boy person is Pajimminy-Crimminy Unusual. He is maybe as dangerous as – ” Brian had to swallow hard and cough before he managed to say – “a *swamp*

monster... I would like him to be – please and thank you – locked up at once.”

At this point, the Tweed-Faced Boy said, “Oingy-boingy boo. I am sooo Unusual!” And then he wriggled his fingers as Unusually as he could.

Dr. P'Klawz studied the Tweed-Faced Boy. “A very serious case and definitely infectious, too. Has he licked or bitten you, Mr. Smith?”

Brian forgot he was meant to be called Mr. Smith and so he didn't answer. The Tweed-Faced Boy had to stamp on the slippers Ginalolobrigida had tied to Brian's hooves. "Ah. Yes. I am Mr. Smith. No. I have not been litten or bicked."

"Good. Then I will lock him up tight and squish the Unusualness right out of him until he is miserable all over... I mean, I will make him better." P'Klawz studied Brian's knocking knees – hidden inside Uncle Shawn's trousers. And then P'Klawz studied Brian's really very llama-looking face, hidden under the shadow of his hat. "Mr. Smith, you have an Unusually Long nose..."

"This nose runs in my family," said Brian. And then – being extra brave and clever – he said, "And you, Mr. Doctor P'Klawz, sir, have an Unusually Stripy, Drippy-looking face. Is that hair paint?"

Dr. P'Klawz rubbed at his face with his perfectly white sleeve – which made the sleeve dirty. His head ached, his teeth were *skreeing,* his shins were itching, the inmates were laughing and

175

singing. And Uncle Shawn... As soon as he even thought of Uncle Shawn... *SKREEEEEEE...* Unusually, gargantunormously happy Uncle Shawn... *SKREEEEEEE...* Uncle Shawn who was Pajimminy-Crimminy Unusual!

SKREEEEEEE!!!

P'Klawz had expected Uncle Shawn to be sadder than anyone had ever been when he was locked up, because he was happier than anyone else had ever been when he wasn't locked up. But Uncle Shawn, of course, had spent years practicing how to stay happy and was very good at it. And he was Unusual without even trying. And now he was making the whole Institution more Unusually Happy.

"Perhaps you should come inside – *skreeeeeeeee* – and we can sign all the necessary paperwork. Then I will pop this boy into a nice warm dungeon – I mean, a bedroom with lots of toys and games to make him better." P'Klawz winced and felt woozy.

176

DUNGEON ↓

CHAINS

BUNDLE OF RAGS TO SLEEP UNDER ↓

RAT

CUP OF WATER

BEDROOM ↓

COMFY BED

TEDDY BEAR

HARMONICA - PLAYING RAT

COCOA

(He felt woozy, because at that moment Uncle Shawn was being Especially Gargantunormously Unusual by hopping backward and whistling the Swedish national anthem.)

"Yes, please!" said Brian. "I would love to come inside."

Brian would much rather have been hiding under a quilt, but he knew that he had to help Uncle Shawn, so he went inside the gates, being always careful to let P'Klawz see his front view.

If P'Klawz ever saw his furry big llama bottom and extra set of legs, he would know Brian wasn't a human person. Human people may have big bottoms, but those bottoms are never covered in chocolate-colored fur.

Uncle Shawn looked out of the rattly old dormitory window and grinned and grinned. He watched P'Klawz walking across the exercise yard with a small boy wearing a tweed mask and a human person (with Brian's bottom attached) in one of Bill's hats. He grinned and grinned and grinned.

This grin was big enough, all by itself, to give P'Klawz a stabbing ache in his huge, shiny teeth.

And Uncle Shawn could also see a big black cloud on the horizon, a very low and somehow Unusual cloud... A cloud with llama ears...

Seeing the cloud made him grin even more. 🐾

SQUID IMPRESSION

SECTION EIGHTEEN

In which we get a visit from a famous llama film star. There is a very good impression of a squid by someone called Alice. And both halves of the plan are working...

As P'Klawz led Brian and the Tweed-Faced Boy away, the two gray guards on duty at the gate were just wondering whether they should lock it, even though P'Klawz hadn't told them to, when two glamorous ladies appeared. One of them was holding a small girl by the hand and the other had a stripy, Unusually Grumpy dog on a leash.

"Hello, you most handsome gentlemen in

uniform," said the first lady. "I am Ginalolobrigida Magnifica, the famous Peruvian film star. I am sure you have heard of me." She fluttered her eyelashes which were so long and thick that this caused quite a draft. The taller guard – who was called Peter – sneezed.

As you may have guessed – because you are very clever – this was not a famous film star but Ginalolobrigida Llama wearing some curtains and another of Bill's hats. Guinevere was also dressed in flowery curtains and – like Brian and Ginalolobrigida – she looked like a human person if you only saw her from the front, with her plaited fur arms, wrapped in curtain-material sleeves, and dainty human shoes painted on her hooves.

Between them was Linvizzygirl, her invisible face painted all over with makeup. This made her look like a usual kind of girl.

Guinevere announced, "I am the assistant of

GINALOLOBRIGIDA MAGNIFICA
The famous Peruvian film star

AND HER INCREDIBLY
NORMAL NIECE

HIGHLY
USUAL
CARDIGAN

MAKEUP

EXCITING
HAT

CELEBRITY
LIPSTICK

FAMOUS
CAPE

PINK
GLOVES

GLOVES
KNITTED
BY BILL

SHOES PAINTED
ON HOOVES →

Miss Magnifica and am equally attractive, but I just didn't feel like being a film star. I am above such things and have a degree in physics."

"Get on with it," said Ginalolobrigida.

Guinevere said, "We have come with Miss Magnifica's incredibly normal and usual niece to see your Institution. And I have brought my dog.

Who is completely usual."

"Woof," said her dog.

"He is a Lithuanian Badger Spaniel. They are very rare. And stripy. And fat," explained Ginalolobrigida.

"Woof," said her dog, again. (He was, of course, Badger Bill, walking on all fours and pretending he couldn't speak, even though he wanted to say, "I am not fat. I am just the right size for a healthy young badger. And why have

GINALOLOBRIGIDA MAGNIFICA's *glamorous* ASSISTANT

AND HER LITHUANIAN BADGER SPANIEL

I got the most horrible disguise?")

Peter and the other gray guard, Hamish, didn't look closely at the two glamorous ladies, because their mothers had taught them it was rude to stare. And the guards didn't pay any attention to the little girl, who was all dressed up in a big cardigan and had pink gloves over her invisible hands and brown tights covering her invisible legs. Here and there, where her makeup had rubbed off, there seemed to be no girl at all, but the guards didn't notice because Guinevere and Ginalolobrigida were keeping them busy with compliments.

"You look so handsome in your cap."

"Are there any Unusual babies? A guard would have to be extremely courageous to deal with an Unusual baby."

"Your boots make you look very intelligent."

And so the guards walked them around the Institution grounds, never looking at the llamas from the side and never casting a glance at the little girl covered in makeup or the stripy dog.

As soon as the guards were out of earshot, Bill whispered to the llamas, "I'm not fat and *remember the plan*. We have to get inside the buildings."

Uncle Shawn caught sight of Guinevere and Ginalolobrigida and Linvizzygirl and his best friend Bill through the window and smiled to himself and then pretended to be a very tall rabbit, hippety-hopping across the floor while everyone laughed.

Then Uncle Shawn held up his hands, "Shooooosh. I need your help. Hani, Angus, Hughie, Margaret, Liam, all of you, I need you to remember what you were like before you were brought here. I need you to remember all the Unusual things you did. You there!" He pointed at the very smallest inmate. "What did *you* do?"

The smallest inmate looked a bit nervous. "I used to like hanging over the edge of my bed with

WHEEEE!

my head upside down and saying, *Wheeee.*"

"Wonderful! Then you should try doing that now."

The smallest inmate lay over the edge of the mattress platform with his head upside down and said, quietly at first, "*Wheeee.*" And then when Uncle Shawn grinned at him and clapped his hands, the smallest inmate suddenly said, "I've remembered! I am not Inmate Number 4333. I am Jamie! And my mum is

WHOOOOO!!!!! WHEEEE! WHAAA!

Katie! And she is somewhere in here, too! And I can go, WHOOOOOOO! WHEEEEE! WHAAAAAA!"

All the other inmates cheered and Uncle Shawn asked, "And what about you, Hani?"

Hani said, "I would pretend I was a parrot and I would only speak in a parrot voice until someone would give me a peanut."

"Perfect!" said Uncle Shawn. "Try it now!"

After that all the inmates were calling out ways

they had of being Unusual. Soon the whole dormitory was full of people pretending to be dragons, or burping "This Badger's Gotta Move," or farting and pretending that their farts were rocket powered and running up and down. And Inmate Alice pretended to be a squid. She looked more like a squid than a lot of squids. She was amazing.

Uncle Shawn whistled for quiet. "What I need now is for everyone in all the dormitories to remember who they really are and what their Unusualnesses are. Then we will all be as Unusual as we can together and Doctor P'Klawz will have the worst brain ache ever and his shins will itch as much as underpants full of sand and his teeth will sound like millions of fingernails on blackboards. So after three we'll shout to them, 'REMEMBER WHO YOU ARE! REMEMBER YOUR UNUSUALNESS!' And then we'll shout, 'AFTER THREE, BE UNUSUAL!'"

So everyone in Uncle Shawn's dormitory

shouted together, "REMEMBER WHO YOU ARE! REMEMBER YOUR UNUSUALNESS!"

They waited for a tiny while. Then Uncle Shawn conducted everyone in his dormitory by waving his arms and together they all shouted, "AFTER THREE, BE UNUSUAL!"

"ONE!"

"TWO!"

"THREE!"

Suddenly the whole Institution was full of the noises of Unusualness.

Little girls and boys were squeaking like bats and tooting like trumpets, and inmates were raspberry blowing and imitating queasy camels. Jamie could hear his mum, Katie, making the sounds of sharks on holiday – the way she used to when they were having fun at bath time.

There were sounds no one had ever heard before because they were PAJIMMINY-CRIMMINY UNUSUAL. 🐾

SECTION NINETEEN

*In which we learn the right way to wear a
guard's cap and the gray guards finally get to
have some fun – even though they still can't play
table tennis. And Uncle Shawn's plan and Bill's
plan are almost ready to meet in the middle.*

Henry Witherbottom could hear all the Unusualness from where he was sitting in the guards' recreation room – which only had three jigsaw puzzles (with pieces missing) and a table-tennis table with no net and no paddles because P'Klawz didn't want the gray guards to have fun. The other guards heard the Unusual noises, too. But

189

Henry ignored them and kept on reading his book about how to grow rhubarb (he liked rhubarb). He also very gently sang "Old MacDonald Had a Farm" in chicken noises.

"*Bock-bock bock-bock*
Bock bock bock
Bock-bock bock-bock bock."

And then he smiled and tipped his hat back so that he could feel more relaxed and (he thought) look a bit like a sea captain.

The rest of the guards felt much happier after that. They didn't do anything about the Unusualness either. They snoozed, or poured mugs of orange juice and chatted, or knitted socks. One of the guards, called Amanda, did a little dance in her big guard's boots that looked a lot like the Clog and Smock Dance that Uncle Shawn had invented. When she'd finished, some of the other guards clapped. It was the best day they could remember having in the Institution.

ALL KINDS OF UNUSUALNESS

Wobbling Burping

Dancing

In all of the dormitories, all kinds of Unusualness continued.

But in Uncle Shawn's dormitory, everyone was quiet and still, because Guard 5555 and Guard 5557 had marched in to take Uncle Shawn away. They looked very fierce and frowned a lot.

They frowned even more when Uncle Shawn said, "Ah, how wonderful! I have been waiting for you. Now let's see if we can find out more about squishing..."

Guard 5555 wasn't used to people being happy around him, so he poked Uncle Shawn in the ribs. Guard 5557 laughed. They were horrible people.

And they led Uncle Shawn away.

While he walked between them, Uncle Shawn thought, "I know that my friends have a plan... I just have to wait. And then they will rescue me. I do not want to be squished, not even a tiny bit... I wonder what will happen? If I am rescued, it will be the best day ever! If I am squished, it will not be good at all."

Uncle Shawn hoped that Unusualness could save him.

"It isn't much of a plan, but I think it is enough of a plan."

They marched on.

Of course, all this Unusualness was making Dr. P'Klawz feel Unusually Ill. He was still with Brian in disguise (and Brian's big llama bottom,

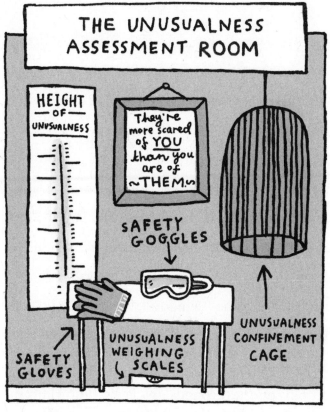

THE UNUSUALNESS
ASSESSMENT ROOM

HEIGHT
—OF—
UNUSUALNESS

They're more scared of YOU than you are of ~THEM.~

SAFETY GOGGLES

SAFETY GLOVES

UNUSUALNESS WEIGHING SCALES

UNUSUALNESS CONFINEMENT CAGE

which wasn't disguised at all) and the Tweed-Faced Boy. P'Klawz was trying to lead them to the Unusualness Assessment Room, but his shins were so prickly and hot that his socks were smoldering. His teeth sounded like a navy full of mice singing sea shanties and pulling on pulleys that needed oiling.

"This way – *skreeeeee*. If you would follow – *skreeeeeeee* – me," managed P'Klawz.

It was lucky that there was such a din, because otherwise the noise of Brian's knees knocking would have been as loud as coconuts rolling down a cobbled street. The deeper he went into the Institution, the more he worried. The Tweed-Faced Boy rubbed one of Brian's ears to make him feel braver.

Through the windows, Brian could see Guinevere and Ginalolobrigida Llama, and their shapely, undisguised llama bottoms, being given a tour of the grounds by Peter and Hamish, the guards. (They were all looking at the garbage shed. It was the prettiest part of the whole Institution. The guards often came and looked at it for hours.)

Brian did some quick thinking before P'Klawz caught sight of the llama bottoms. "Perhaps please may we get away from the Unusualness

MAGNIFICENT
BEAUTY SPOTS
FROM THE INSTITUTION
OF MAXIMUM SECURITY
AND UNUSUALNESS
CURING

RAT EATING POTATO
PEEL ON CANTEEN FLOOR

DRAIN OUTSIDE
B BLOCK

BROOM CUPBOARD IN
EAST CORRIDOR

STAIN ON CEILING OF
DORMITORY 15

THE WONDERFUL
GARBAGE SHED

and maybe climb a tower to be far away from it?"

"*SKREEEEE!*" said P'Klawz. "I mean, yes. I have an towice in my offer. I mean, an office in my ***SKREEEEEEE***. Come with me."

And P'Klawz almost ran towards the curly, twirly staircase that wound up the tower.

SKREEEEEEEEEEEEE. 🐾

SECTION TWENTY

*In which (in case you are wondering) we return
to the Unusual cloud rolling and rumbling along
towards the Institution... The cloud has llama
ears sticking out of it and, if you listen very
carefully, is giggling in a Peruvian accent.*

While Unusualness was breaking out all over, a large black cloud rolled along the road that led to the Institution. Hamish and Peter, the gate guards, didn't notice it, because they were on their tour with Guinevere and Ginalolobrigida and, at that very moment, were discussing how often the drains got blocked.

So the cloud rolled silently in through the gate, which had been left wide open. It rolled across the exercise yard and then leaned against the wall of P'Klawz's high gray tower.

And then – and I'm sure you will agree this was Pajimminy-Crimminy Unusual – the cloud began to climb the tower...

This was because Carlos had agreed to walk all the way to the Institution inside a cloud made of spiders all holding hands. They had lots of eyes and told him which way to go by tickling his whiskers.

That was why the cloud had llama ears.

I wonder what the spiders will do next...? 🐾

SECTION TWENTY-ONE

In which there is some Unusually Peculiar singing and some Unusually Wobbly dancing, which will hide our view of an Unusually Lovely garbage shed. And also – oh no! A bit of Bill's plan is missing!

As you will remember, Ginalolobrigida was pretending to be the famous Peruvian film star Ginalolobrigida Magnifica, and Guinevere was pretending to be her assistant. Linvizzygirl was pretending to be a usual kind of little girl: skipping and pointing at clouds, and trying not to scratch her nose or lick her lips because that would wipe off the makeup that was covering up her invisibility.

Poor Badger Bill was still having to pretend he was a Lithuanian Badger Spaniel. The dog collar was rubbing his neck and people were being very rude about him having a large nose for a dog. And in his big, golden heart, Bill was really worried about his best friend, Uncle Shawn. "Oh, Uncle Shawn, I hope you are OK and they haven't already squished you."

"What was that?" asked Peter the guard – who was by now very much in love with Ginalolobrigida.

"Woof. Grrrr..." said Bill.

Ginalolobrigida laughed in her best ladylike, film-star way. "Oh, sometimes it's as if he's talking. He may be tubby, but he is so clever. Ow!" She didn't mean to say "Ow!" but Bill had kicked one of her legs.

Hamish the guard, who was very much in love with Guinevere, said dreamily, "We should really go back to the gates now – it's not allowed for strangers to be in the Institution."

PETER + GINA LOLOBRIGIDA
TRU LUV
HAMISH + GUINEVERE 4 EVA!

"WOOF," said Bill. This was to remind the llama ladies that they needed to remember the plan. "WOOF!"

"I will bend down to listen to my dog's silly, tubby woofing," declared Guinevere. "Because I am not a selfish actress, I have time to listen to all the creatures of the world." And she lowered her head so that Bill could whisper to her.

Not to be outdone, Ginalolobrigida said, "As the world's most famous and gorgeous actress, I help orphans and dolphins and all kinds of creatures. I also shall listen to the silly, stripy dog."

Bill whispered to them both, "I am not tubby."

"We are just pretending," Ginalolobrigida whispered back.

Bill growled, "Linvizzygirl and I have to get away. Distract the guards. We have to rescue Uncle Shawn before he gets squished! WOOF!"

So Guinevere stood up straight and announced, "And now, Ginalolobrigida Magnifica will sing for you!"

"What?" squeaked Ginalolobrigida.

"Yes! She will sing one of her famous songs."

Ginalolobrigida, of course, didn't really know any songs. "Why don't *you* sing, my assistant?"

"No. You are the famous film star. I am just the assistant."

Peter and Hamish clapped their hands. "Oh,

wonderful! A real Peruvian film star's real Peruvian singing."

So Ginalolobrigida decided to do her best. "I will sing a wonderful traditional song of Peru – 'Mi Corazón Está Aplastado'."

Not to be outdone, Guinevere added, "And I will dance!"

"Oooh..." sighed the two guards. They leaned romantically against the garbage shed as Guinevere began wiggling back and forth – without revealing her llama bottom.

WIGGLING

LLAMA BOTTOM
(hidden)

Ginalolobrigida continued, "'Mi Corazón Está Aplastado' means 'My Heart is Squished.' It is a sad song about a lovely llama – I mean, lady – whose heart is broken by a cruel man in a hat."

Ginalolobrigida started to sing. She was not exactly the best singer in the world, or even near the garbage shed, but she hit lots of very high, wibbly notes and rolled her eyes very impressively.

HIGH, WIBBLY NOTES

The guards were astonished and watched her every move – when they weren't looking at Guinevere's alarming dancing.

Bill and Linvizzygirl sneaked away.

"Oh no! I didn't remember my lock-picking tools," said Bill.

"Do you own lock-picking tools?" asked Linvizzygirl, quickly rubbing off her makeup and throwing away her cardigan as they ran.

"No..." sighed Bill. "I don't even know how to pick a lock. This bit is a gap where there is no plan!"

But then Bill saw the window of the guards' recreation room and he invented a new piece of plan, just like that! He was a resourceful badger.

By this time, Linvizzygirl was invisible again, which made her feel much safer, since she was so close to P'Klawz and his nastiness.

Bill jumped as high in the air as he could – which wasn't very high, because he only had short legs and was still pretending to be a Lithuanian Badger Spaniel. Fortunately, after about five minutes of breathless jumping, Bill heard Henry Witherbottom shout to the other gray guards, "Look! A puppy! Aw!"

Moments later, a squash of guards ran round to a side door, opened it and raced to where Bill was lying on the ground, getting his breath back.

"Oh, look! He's lying down. Maybe he needs

hugs. Maybe he needs tickles. Maybe he needs a biscuit. Who has dog food?" called the guards as they all tried to pick Bill up and stroke his fur and tickle his nose.

Bill thought, "This is what it must feel like when you are the parcel in Pass the Parcel. Which is why no one ever volunteers to be the parcel..."

Henry Witherbottom – who had always wanted a dog – rubbed Bill's ears and said, "He needs love! Let's take him inside to our room!"

And that was how Bill got into the Institution. And Linvizzygirl invisibly sneaked in after him. 🐾

SECTION TWENTY-TWO

In which— Oh, but what has happened to Uncle Shawn? He was taken away to be squished and maybe that has already happened! We can hardly look…

Uncle Shawn was inside the Squishing Room!

He was trying not to look at the Squishing Machine, because it was the most terrible and horrible and blood-curdling thing anyone had ever seen. Guard 5555 was polishing its dials and Guard 5557 was adjusting its straps.

Uncle Shawn wanted to hold Bill's paw and maybe have a hug. He didn't want to be in this dreadful room, with this dreadful machine.

He really hoped that Bill was coming for him and that everyone else was helping.

"I just have to keep delaying things for as long as possible," thought Uncle Shawn. He studied 5555 and 5557, and noticed that 5557 had a smear on his boots and 5555's hat wasn't straight.

"I will start with that," he told himself.

Wonky hat

Then Uncle Shawn said to 5557, "5555 is tilting his hat Unusually to one side." He knew that people like 5555 and 5557 wanted everyone and everything to be perfect all the time, but Uncle Shawn also knew that being perfect is impossible. "And 5557 has an Unusual mark on his boot, doesn't he, 5555? Maybe he was trying to spread jam on his toecap. That would be Very Unusual, wouldn't it?"

The guards ignored him. But they looked at each other with suspicion as they prepared the great big gargantunormous Squishing Machine.

"Oh, Bill – do be quite quick, please," thought Uncle Shawn.

Let's hope Bill gets there soon. Otherwise – *SQUISHING!* 🐾

SECTION TWENTY-THREE

In which Carlos Llama stands in the middle of the Institution exercise yard. And we wonder what he is going to do.

In the Institution exercise yard, Carlos shook his head and a large, cheerful spider bounced down on a delicate rope of spider silk.

It was Claude.

211

CLAUDE
the spider

He slowly let out more silk, then landed on the ground and trotted away on seven of his legs. He was waving goodbye with the other one.

This was Pajimminy-Crimminy Unusual.

Very soon, Carlos Llama is going to blow his whistle and all kinds of things are going to happen all at once.

I'm not sure that I can wait…

Tickling hand

Tickled Badger

SECTION TWENTY-FOUR

In which Bill gets tickled and Brian nearly loses his gloves (which is a problem because they are pretending to be his hands ...) and both halves of the plan join together. I do hope this means that everyone is all right and no one gets squished!

While the guards were taking turns to tickle Bill's tummy and Linvizzygirl was searching the Institution, P'Klawz led Brian and the Tweed-Faced Boy up the twirly stairs to his office and took them inside.

But – oh no – after so much twirly climbing, Brian could feel his arms (which were made of his own

213

PLAITS COMING UNDONE

GLOVES WORKING LOOSE

plaited llama fur, you will remember) slowly coming undone and his gloves were working loose. His knees knocked like all the postmen in the world. His borrowed hat was getting in his eyes and here he was – trapped up in a high tower with the nasty, nasty P'Klawz! "If the plan does not work, I will be squished for sure," he thought. "Oh, I do not think I will like being squished..."

Brian and the Tweed-Faced Boy were waiting for Carlos to blow the whistle, which would let everyone know that both halves of the plan were going to meet in the middle. "Maybe the whistle has already blown but I have not heard it," Brian thought. "Maybe my ears have stopped working... Oh no. *EMERGENCIA!* My ears are broken."

But Brian kept on pretending to be a human person. He tried to look around the office as if he wasn't scared. He stared at the velvety thick black carpet under the desk and the framed certificates P'Klawz had on his walls. "I am not afraid of the certificates," Brian thought. "They are silly pieces of paper and do not scare me at all." He felt proud for a moment and nearly grinned.

P'Klawz sat behind his desk as if he would much rather be hiding underneath it. He had spent many, many evenings drawing his certificates on his computer and then printing them out on special paper. He tried to get his squeaking teeth to smile, but the result sounded like a thousand shrews on rusty roller skates. He scratched his shins and he said to Brian, "That certificate is from – *SKREEEEEEEEEEEE* – the University of Sidney."

"Shouldn't that be Sydney?" asked Brian – glad that he could hear.

P'Klawz frowned. "And that is my certificate for underwater swimming – SKREEEEEEEEEEEE – with crocodiles and – SKREEEEEEEEE-

215

EEE – that one says I am really a real doctor."

Brian could feel his stuffed glove hands getting closer and closer to falling off. But he kept talking, because he really was a brave llama. "And where, please, is this Knowledge College?"

"It's … um … in France… No, Spain… No, Bolton… No – *SKREEEEEEEEEEEE*!"

Meanwhile, the Tweed-Faced Boy watched the office door open all by itself and then he watched footprints appear in the office carpet and then he saw the door to the cupboard that held all the Institution's keys swing open… He knew this was Linvizzygirl, taking the keys to set free all the inmates, including Uncle Shawn.

But – oh no! – the hinges of the cupboard door needed oiling and they squeaked. *Skreeeeee.*

"What was that?" asked P'Klawz.

"I think it was your teeth," said Brian, being very clever.

For a long moment, P'Klawz stared at Brian in a

216

DR. P'KLAWZ's
CERTIFICATES

COMPLETELY GENUINE
ASTRONAUT
CERTIFICATE

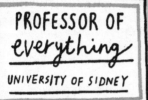
PROFESSOR OF
everything
UNIVERSITY OF SIDNEY

UNDERWATER
SWIMMING
1,000 Meters

FULLY QUALIFIED
Wizard

TALLEST
MAN
IN THE WORLD

PLUMBING
and HEATING
Specialist
KNOWLEDGE COLLEGE

QUALIFIED
REAL DOCTOR,
HONESTLY.

suspicious way. This made Brian's fur go all hot and frightened, but it meant that P'Klawz didn't notice the twirling dust and the little breeze of air that showed Linvizzygirl had left the room. Then P'Klawz said, "Are you sure you would not like to stay in my Institution as well as this Horribly Unusual boy...? You really do look as if you need squishing. I have never met a human person with such a long nose."

And this was so scary that Brian nearly just yelled, "I am a llama in disguise and I want to go home! Only I have to help rescue Uncle Shawn because he is the nicest human person in the world and you are not to squish him, so there!"

But then...

Brian heard Carlos blow his whistle and suddenly lots of PAJIMMINY-CRIMMINY UNUSUAL things happened all at once.

Because this was the part where everyone's plans met in the middle! 🐾

Whistle

SECTION TWENTY-FIVE

In which we learn what happens to Guinevere and Ginalolobrigida when Carlos blows his whistle.

Next to the garbage shed, Guinevere Llama was tap dancing (sort of) and Ginalolobrigida Llama had just repeated verse sixteen of "Mi Corazón Está Aplastado." The guards, Hamish and Peter, were watching and listening with tears in their eyes, because they were very moved and also some of Ginalolobrigida's high notes were painful. The guards didn't speak Spanish, so they didn't know that Ginalolobrigida had run out of verses to make up about being heartbroken and wearing her sad

219

hat of flowers and misery. Verse sixteen was just a recipe for fruitcake.

Then the whistle blew.

CARLOS

At once Guinevere shiggled and wriggled and squiggled until all her disguise had fallen off! She stood in front of the guards, looking exactly like the highly intelligent llama she was.

Ginalolobrigida nearly hit a high C, then

bowed and bowed until her disguise fell off and she was revealed as – yes! – a fabulously gorgeous llama with many skills!

"Ha!" shouted both the llamas, just as they had practiced. "We are the Most Unusual llamas you will ever meet!" And they shook their llama bottoms Unusually.

But this just made Peter and Hamish clap their hands and shout, "If this is Unusualness, we want more!" and also "You are the most beautiful and talented llamas we've ever met!"

To be fair, neither of the guards had met any llamas before.

Guinevere and Ginalolobrigida had expected the guards would run away, but instead the llamas ended up signing autographs and chatting about being wonderful.

This kept the guards just as busy as running away would have, and Guinevere and Ginalolobrigida enjoyed it much more. 🐾

MANY, MANY KEYS

SECTION TWENTY-SIX

In which we learn what happens to
Linvizzygirl when Carlos blows his whistle.

Linvizzygirl had run down from the tower and was unlocking all of the doors she could find. This took her a long time because there were many, many keys and many, many doors and she didn't know which key fit which door. She was meant to find Uncle Shawn and set him free.

And then the whistle blew.

Inmates were running and skipping about as Linvizzygirl unlocked another door and another, but still *she couldn't find Uncle Shawn*! 🐾

POORLY BADGER

BISCUIT CRUMBS

SECTION TWENTY-SEVEN

In which we learn what happens to Badger
Bill when Carlos blows his whistle.

In the guards' recreation room, Bill had been tickled so much that he felt a bit sick. He had also been fed a lot of biscuits.

And then the whistle blew.

At once Bill stood up very tall and announced, "Behold! I am … um … Captain Stripe Nose the badger pirate!"

The guards stopped knitting and telling stories and stared at him.

Then a small guard, who had just dropped all

his stitches in a very complicated sock because of this new excitement, asked, "If you are a pirate, why don't you have a pirate hat?"

Bill grabbed a newspaper and quickly folded himself a small pirate hat. Then he started again, "Behold! I am Captain Stripe Nose!"

Some of the guards clapped and called out, "A talking dog, what fun!" Others backed away, in case they caught Unusualness.

Bill shouted, "I am not a talking dog. I am a talking badger!"

"Oh dear," murmured one of the guards. "A dog that thinks it's a badger. That's Highly Unusual."

Bill tried to look dangerous. "If any of you touch me, you will become Unusual! So stay back!"

All the guards had touched Bill when they tickled his tummy. Some of the guards cheered and said things like, "Well, I feel better than I

CAPTAIN STRIPE NOSE
the
FEARSOME BADGER PIRATE

100 PERCENT CERTIFIED PIRATE
(NOT BADGER BILL)

EYES GLARING LIKE A PIRATE'S

SMALL EMERGENCY PIRATE HAT (MADE OF NEWSPAPER)

TEETH-GLEAMING SMILE LIKE A PIRATE'S

KNEES BENT AT A PIRATICAL ANGLE

HANDS PLACED ON HIPS TO LOOK BIGGER AND MORE LIKE A SEA DOG

have in ages. Maybe Unusualness is good for you," or "He's a lovely dog. I wonder what kind he is?" or "I think I'm already Unusual. It's making my knees tingle. And I like tingly knees."

This wasn't quite what Bill had expected, but while the guards were discussing whether they were Unusual, Badger Bill ran away.

He stepped into a long, gray, nasty-feeling corridor. Bill really needed to find his friend Uncle Shawn, because he missed him in all of his paws and whiskers and wanted to be sure that he was smiling and safe. But where was Uncle Shawn? 🐾

VERY WHITE
↩ UNDERPANTS

SECTION TWENTY-EIGHT

In which we don't learn what happens to Uncle Shawn when Carlos blows the whistle. It might be much too scary, or much too sad, or much too Unusual. So we won't say what is happening to Bill's best friend, behind the big iron door in the basement with a sign on it that says Squishing Room. Oh... No...

Up and down the passageways and corridors went Badger Bill, looking for his best friend. He ran up and down and in and out.

But Uncle Shawn was nowhere to be seen.

Bill even searched the attic rooms, where P'Klawz kept his perfectly clean clothes. He found rows of shiny shoes and stacks of fresh underpants from the Brilliant White Underpants Company. (Which was founded by a lady from Aberdeen, called Ellie Smith, whose mother told her always to wear fresh underpants when she went out.)

But there was no sign of Uncle Shawn.

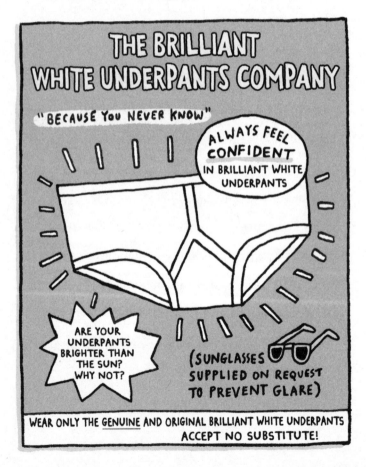

THE BRILLIANT WHITE UNDERPANTS COMPANY

"BECAUSE YOU NEVER KNOW"

ALWAYS FEEL CONFIDENT IN BRILLIANT WHITE UNDERPANTS

ARE YOUR UNDERPANTS BRIGHTER THAN THE SUN? WHY NOT?

(SUNGLASSES SUPPLIED ON REQUEST TO PREVENT GLARE)

WEAR ONLY THE GENUINE AND ORIGINAL BRILLIANT WHITE UNDERPANTS ACCEPT NO SUBSTITUTE!

Then Bill reached the very last dormitory. It was empty.

"Oh, Uncle Shawn, I will never let you go somewhere as nasty as this, not ever again," he said to no one.

Bill was tired and scared and didn't know what to do. "I can't see Uncle Shawn anywhere," he thought.

And then...

"But I don't have to see him!" Bill shouted. He pelted out of the dormitory and into the Institution's maze of hallways and stairs. "I can track him by scent!"

Bill concentrated really hard and remembered that Uncle Shawn's scent was a mixture of friendliness and toffee and seaside and wibbly hair and UNUSUALNESS.

And Bill's sensitive badger nose sniffed about really carefully...

There...

No, there…

And here…

And here – this way!

Bill found the scent trail left behind by Uncle Shawn and began to follow it. He could also smell two human people with nastiness running all the way through them, like dirty socks hiding in a jelly roll.

He just hoped that he would get to Uncle Shawn in time.

We all do. 🐾

SECTION TWENTY-NINE

In which you now know what everyone did when Carlos blew his whistle. SO LET'S FIND OUT WHAT HAPPENED NEXT! (EVEN IF IT'S A BIT SCARY.)

Up in the high gray tower, Brian knew the whistle was the signal to start THE DEFEAT P'KLAWZ AND RESCUE UNCLE SHAWN PLAN.

But Brian was looking into P'Klawz's horrible shiny eyes and he felt as if his hooves were glued to the spot.

P'Klawz's teeth were rattling and grinding like pebbles in a rusty dishwasher because the Institution was now so full of Unusualness. He was hissing at Brian, "Your nose is Unusual and – *SKREEEEEEEEE* – your voice sounds Unusual and—" P'Klawz didn't say anything else, because just then Brian's pretend left hand fell to the floor. *Splaff.*

Then Brian's other hand fell off. *Sploff.*

And Brian nearly ran away down the whirly stairs, but then he thought of Uncle Shawn and Bill and all his friends and he said, "I don't know what you are talking about, Mr. Doctor, sir."

SKREEEEEEEEEEEEE went P'Klawz's teeth. Loose hands were Very Unusual.

Then – according to the plan – Brian turned round and wiggled his big llama bottom.

"SKREEEEEEEEEEEEE – stop that at once! You are turning into a camel!"

Brian turned round again and made sure to sound very calm and puzzled when he said, "I do not know what you are talking about. I am a human person."

232

"SKREEEEEEEEEEEEE."

While Brian was speaking, the noise coming from the inmates who had escaped from the dormitories was getting more and more Unusual.

And clattering up the tower's twirly stairs came Guinevere and Ginalolobrigida, singing a selection of the best verses from "Mi Corazón Está Aplastado" and joined by Hamish and Peter, who were having more fun than they'd ever had in their lives.

At the sight of singing and dancing llamas, P'Klawz's teeth ground against each other even harder.

SKREEEEEEEEEEE!

And sneaking into the office came Linvizzygirl. She picked several of P'Klawz's certificates off the wall and held them up with her invisible hands and made them dance.

This was all Too Unusual for P'Klawz. He dived

– SKREEEEEEEEE!

– under his desk to hide.

That was when the black, velvety carpet under his desk wooshed up and swallowed Dr. P'Klawz up into a big velvety lump. Which was Pajimminy-Crimminy Unusual!

The spiders, under the command of clever Claude, had flattened themselves out – all holding hands – like a carpet under P'Klawz's desk and now they had surrounded him.

From inside the spiders everyone could hear P'Klawz's teeth –

SKREEEEEEEE! 🐾

BADGER IN DESPAIR

SECTION THIRTY

In which while the World Association of Spiders (Pandrumdroochit Branch) is tickling and holding P'Klawz, we wonder who is rescuing Uncle Shawn? We need him to be safe and sound and not squished. Please remember to look away when I tell you to.

Badger Bill's paws were shaking. He had followed the scent of Uncle Shawn down into the lowest level of the Institution. He could smell unhappiness going all the way towards a great big metal door that looked very cruel.

On the outside of the door, someone had painted: **SQUISHING ROOM.**

Bill put his paw to the metal and it felt as cold as P'Klawz's heart.

The door had a huge handle, which Bill could just reach if he stood on tip-paws, but it wouldn't turn. It was locked.

Uncle Shawn's scent led right to this door. Bill didn't know what to do. He felt like a very small badger indeed.

But then he heard a laugh from the other side of the door.

Whose laugh was it?

Yes!

It was Uncle Shawn's!

"Nobody can laugh if they've been squished," thought Bill, and his chest felt sparkly.

He put his sensitive badger ear against the door and listened.

Bill could hear – very faintly – Uncle Shawn saying to someone, "I don't think that it would be safe for you to switch on the Squishing Machine when you are turning Unusual."

"I'm not Unusual!" shouted a growly, meaty voice. "Guard 5555 is the one who's Unusual!"

"No, I'm not!" yelled an even more growly and meaty voice. "It's not my fault that my mum and dad called me Wilberforce Smidgely Brown. Now I'm called 5555 – that's not Unusual at all! What's *your* proper name?"

"5557 is my proper name – the other one was wrong!"

Bill began to smile. "Uncle Shawn has been getting them all mixed up."

Bill rubbed his ears to help himself think. Then he had just the right idea. He put his handsome and stripy badger nose against the metal of the door and said, "I am Doctor P'Klawz! Release the prisoner at once!"

Of course, Bill didn't sound like P'Klawz, even when the guards were hearing his voice through a thick metal door. In fact Guard 5555 – or Wilberforce Smidgely Brown, as his mum would have called him – shouted, "You're not Doctor P'Klawz! You don't sound a bit like him!"

But now Uncle Shawn would know that Bill was outside the metal door, waiting to rescue him!

Bill scraped his claws along the iron surface of the door, so that they went *SKKKRRREEEE*. And he said, "I am Doctor P'Klawz. That's the noise of my teeth."

HOW TO MAKE THE NOISE OF DR. P'KLAWZ'S TEETH: A GUIDE

SANDPAPERING PEBBLES   NAILS ON BLACKBOARD   SCRAPE CLAWS ALONG IRON DOOR

Bill heard 5557 say, "That does sound like Doctor P'Klawz's teeth... Maybe we should take this inmate back to the dormitory."

And then he heard Uncle Shawn say, "Take me back? Without squishing me? That sounds Unusual. I think 5557 may be turning Unusual. What do you think, Wilberforce Smidgely?" And then he said very loudly, "I bet you're both so Unusual that if you opened the door right now, you'd think you could see a badger singing and dancing."

"Oh, goodness. I've never danced in public," thought Bill. "I suppose I shall just have to try."

As 5555 and 5557 unlocked the big locks on the Squishing Room door, Bill got ready. His feet didn't feel like dancing at all – they wanted to run away. The door swung open and there stood the huge Guard 5555 and the huger Guard 5557.

Bill felt shy. But then he saw Uncle Shawn's friendly, wise face in the shadows of the room. And so he hopped a bit and then he skipped and – finally – Bill danced the way he did in his room when he was by himself and no one could see.

And he sang:

"*This badger's gotta move,*

This badger's in the groove,

This badger's super fine,

This badger's dancing, dancing, dancing all the time."

Guard 5555 turned a funny shade of green. "A singing and dancing badger!"

Guard 5557's legs went wibbly. "Lawks. I am Unusual."

HOW TO DANCE
"THIS BADGER'S GOTTA MOVE"

Then they both fainted.

And Bill was almost enjoying his dancing too much to notice. But he did notice when he'd danced all the way into the Squishing Room and Uncle Shawn cheered, "Hazoo! Hazzay! Hazzee!" And Uncle Shawn held out his arms as wide as wide so he could hug him and said, "Bill! Wonderful Bill! You had a plan!"

CENSORED

**LOOK AWAY NOW!
DO NOT TRY TO LOOK AT
THE SQUISHING MACHINE –
IT IS TOO GARGANTUNORMOUSLY
HORRIBLE FOR ANYONE TO SEE.**

Uncle Shawn stood between Bill and the squishing machine so he couldn't see it, and he hugged Bill with the biggest hug there has ever been.

Bill said, "You had a plan, Uncle Shawn!"

"I only had enough plan to last until about now. Do you have any more?"

"No, not really," said Bill, feeling worried again – even though he was pleased in all of his fur to see Uncle Shawn. "Oh, Uncle Shawn, I'm so sorry to have let them take you away. I missed you gargantunormously. We all did."

"But it was the right thing to do, Bill. It meant you could have a plan and I could have a plan, and our plans could meet in the middle and now we'll defeat P'Klawz. I think. Let's think of more plan while we run! This will be marvelous – if we don't all end up being squished!"

They had one more hug and then they ran. Faster than Augusto Llama. 🐾

EVACUATING SPIDERS

SECTION THIRTY-ONE

In which Badger Bill and Uncle Shawn think planning thoughts as they run up the twirly stairs to P'Klawz's office. Even though they are both a bit nervous about meeting thousands of spiders. This section contains teeth.

As Badger Bill and Uncle Shawn raced up the steps in the gray tower, they were surprised by a thick, many-legged and many-eyed carpet of spiders – all of them running away from P'Klawz's office. Claude bobbed down from the ceiling and he didn't look happy. But he didn't stop to spin any words out of thread – he just ran after the others.

245

"Hmm," said Uncle Shawn. "I hope all the Unusualness we've made has been enough to defeat P'Klawz already. But—"

SKREEEEEEEE!

Uncle Shawn and Bill crept up the last few steps and peeked round the office door – Uncle Shawn's head peeking up high and Bill's peeking lower.

What they saw was very unpleasant. If I were you, I'd close one eye while you read about it.

P'Klawz – looking as if he had been tickled by thousands of spiders with dirty feet – was standing on his desk and twirling his shiny watch. Brian and Guinevere and Ginalolobrigida and the Tweed-Faced Boy were all staring at it. Linvizzygirl probably was, too, but no one could see her.

P'Klawz was saying, "Ha! My teeth –

SKREEEEEEEEE

– are so loud the spiders couldn't stand the noise.

Now you will all go to
the Squishing Room,
where you will see what
is left of that Pajimminy-
Crimminy Unusual Uncle
Shawn. Then you will
squish the fun out of
each other and then you
will find that fat badger
and squish him, too!"

At this, Uncle Shawn
and Bill stepped into the room. Uncle Shawn
said, "Well, you could have done better and been
kinder. But you chose not to. And Bill is not fat
– he is just right." Uncle Shawn was still holding
Bill's hand, so he felt brave.

P'Klawz ground his teeth in surprise –

SKREEEEEEEE

– but then he twirled the watch towards Bill and

whispered in an oozing type of voice, "Bill, Uncle Shawn is Too Unusual. Help me put him in the Squishing Machine."

Bill stared at the watch and his head started to swim…

But then Bill felt Uncle Shawn squeeze his paw and heard him say, "It is not Unusualness that you hate, P'Klawz – you hate people being themselves and being happy."

P'Klawz kept twirling the watch while his teeth squealed at the sight of Uncle Shawn –

SKREEEEEE.

But Uncle Shawn just stared at P'Klawz's hair.

"Now I remember you – you're Sylvester Pearlyclaws, the world's most terrible person. And I know exactly what will defeat you – two human people who will fill this room up with the biggest happinesses anyone has ever heard of." And Uncle Shawn walked over to the Tweed-Faced Boy

WANTED
DEAD OR ALIVE
OR DEFINITELY TIED UP IN A SECURE BAG

SYLVESTER PEARLYCLAWS

HIGHLY DANGEROUS, HYPNOTIC CRIMINAL

HISTORY OF CRUELTY AND FIBBING
MASTER OF DISGUISE

CRIMES INCLUDE:

STEALING THE EIFFEL TOWER,
CUTTING HOLES IN THE PYRAMIDS,
GIVING THE STATUE OF LIBERTY A
FOOLISH HAT,
ATTEMPTING TO COVER THE MOON
WITH SPIDERS.

CATCH HIM NOW! OR RUN AWAY!

and gently lifted off his mask to reveal a pale, tired-looking usual kind of boy.

There was a little gasp and then running footsteps without feet. Then the boy moved as if he was being hugged very tightly by an invisible girl.

"Oh, Sam," Linvizzygirl's voice said. "There you are."

The sound of his real name stopped the boy being hypnotized and he shouted and laughed, both at once. "Sky, is it you? How did you get to be invisible? That's so clever!"

"Of course it's me, silly! Woohoo! How good to see you!"

"And – woohoo – how good to *not* see you!" said Sam. He had found his sister and didn't have to be the Tweed-Faced Boy anymore, and Sky didn't have to keep her name a secret anymore, either.

The delighted twins produced more happiness

than anyone on earth had ever known. It was such a strong happiness that it tickled everyone's knees and reminded them they needn't look at P'Klawz's watch. Soon, the whole office was full of hugs and smiles and then...

SKREEEEE!

As Uncle Shawn had guessed, this was too much happiness for P'Klawz. With a last

SKREEEEEE EEEEEEEE EEEEEEE EEEEEEE SPOOFFF!

– all of P'Klawz's teeth broke apart into tiny pieces and a big cloud of tooth dust.

And after the dust had settled ... there was no sign of him.

Everyone cheered! 🐾

SECTION THIRTY-TWO

In which everyone gets a happy ending.

No surprises will happen here.

Or maybe only one...

After a while, all of the bricks from the Institution were taken away and used to make houses for the guards and inmates who wanted to stay in Pandrumdroochit. The houses were lined up along a new road called Skreee Avenue.

Henry Witherbottom and some of the others who had been gray guards put on blindfolds so they wouldn't have to see the Squishing Machine and then hit it with hammers until it was nothing but bits. Then they helped to paint a big new village sign that said:

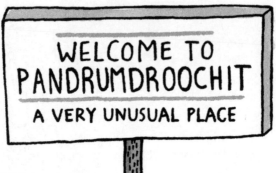

WELCOME TO
PANDRUMDROOCHIT
A VERY UNUSUAL PLACE

On both sides.

And porridge cook Doreen helped to start a new porridge shop next door to the fire station, in the rooms where P'Klawz had once thought nasty thoughts and made nasty plans.

Pandrumdroochit slowly became the friendly place it always had been. And then it kept on getting even more friendly. And Unusual. And every morning, the postman hugged his cat Jemima and she purred like a tractor, and every second Thursday Mrs. MacDonald's cat sat happily in the apple tree, waiting for the firemen.

One warm Sunday, Uncle Shawn invited all of the villagers – new and old – to have a big party down by the seashore near the farm. There were mountains of toasted cheese and pancakes, and there was potato crumble and banana sandwiches and all kinds of wonderful things to eat. Bill didn't cook anything at all – Doreen and the llamas and Uncle Shawn prepared everything so that he could have a rest. And it all may have looked Highly Unusual, but it tasted Unusually Good.

Bill walked on the beach with Uncle Shawn while the villagers paddled and Henry Witherbottom knitted, and Brian and Carlos looked for shells, and Guinevere and Ginalolobrigida had their photographs taken in lots of different hats by Peter and Hamish.

"You know, Bill," said Uncle Shawn, "whenever you want us to do the cooking, or cleaning, you just ask. It was Too Unusual of us all to be so lazy. I myself am excellent at making spam sandwiches, ham sandwiches and jam sandwiches. And custard."

"Maybe we can take turns to cook," said Bill.

"Yes!" cried Uncle Shawn. "I will volunteer to cook for the whole of Limvember!"

"That's not really a month," said Bill.

"It should be." Uncle Shawn smiled and winked.

"But, Uncle Shawn," said Bill, "why were you being so Unusual?"

"I don't know what you mean," said Uncle Shawn.

"Well, you were hopping and sprinkling sugar on paths and making clicking noises."

"I was ant-charming, Bill. I was making sure there would be no ants in the llama barns, drinking the llamas' lemonade. I had to call the ants

Unusual Snaaploo Flavor

Pajimminy-Crimminy Banana Rasberry Crunch Flavor

along new paths that went around the barns. That's not Unusual, is it?"

"No, no." Bill leaned against Uncle Shawn and asked, "But what about when you were hanging upside down from a tree and counting...?"

"Well, someone has to teach the young squirrels how to do acrobatics."

"But why were you throwing jam sandwiches?"

"They were for the wasps to enjoy – so that

they don't get grumpy. Grumpy wasps are a bit stingy. And you never know who else might need a jam sandwich, so it's best to leave some about the place."

"Well, I suppose..." Bill wasn't sure if Uncle Shawn was teasing him. "But what about the times when you were patting the waves and making Unusual noises?"

"Like this, you mean?" Uncle Shawn walked straight into the sea and tickled and patted the water. "I do this so that the sea doesn't get too rough. I am adjusting the waves."

"Oh, I see," said Bill, and he paddled out into the water, too – only up to his very shapely badger knees, because he still couldn't swim. "You were adjusting the sea."

"That's why grown-ups go paddling – to make sure the sea stays the right shape." Uncle Shawn smiled. Then he said, "*BoioioioioioiWoahOOP.*"

Bill was about to ask him why when he felt

hands grab his ankles very quickly and pull him deeper into the water until – oh dear! – he was on his back and bits of sea were going up his stripy nose and then he saw – oh, even more dear! – the face of P'Klawz looking at him from under the water and glaring with his nasty, cruel eyes.

OH NO!

While water gurgled in Bill's ears, he realized that P'Klawz must have run away when no one could see him because of the cloud of powdered teeth. Then he must have hidden himself somewhere. Bill saw in P'Klawz's eyes that it must have been somewhere with lots of room to get angrier than ever.

Bill was holding his breath, but he couldn't for much longer.

(And P'Klawz really did have a certificate for underwater swimming.)

But Bill couldn't swim! Not at all!

EMERGENCIA!

With his poor frightened head underwater, Bill heard Uncle Shawn call out, "*BooWOOooo-AAAhbWahWupWup. BoiboiOOOOoioioip!*" And he felt Uncle Shawn catch hold of his arms and start pulling them.

But with P'Klawz still pulling his feet, this meant Bill was not just underwater, but being stretched underwater! And he could see P'Klawz was smiling with no teeth and saying in a bubbly voice, "You made my teeth ethplode. You ruined my planth! Revenge!"

Then out of the thick, dark water, there appeared a gargantunormous pair of eyes. The eyes winked at Bill as if they had met before. (They had.) Then the eyes stared very hard at P'Klawz.

And P'Klawz saw them and said in a bubbly voice, "Ahhhh!"

P'Klawz let go of Bill and then the fake doctor started to swim much faster than he did on the day when he won his only real certificate.

Uncle Shawn's strong hands pulled Bill up out of the water and patted his back and smoothed his ears. "You're safe now, Bill."

"Oh, Uncle Shawn, Uncle Shawn!" coughed Bill. "I've seen those eyes before! They told me a joke!"

And Uncle Shawn laughed. "Of course. Those are the eyes of my good friend Mr. Hubb, who is a whale. We often have chats in Whalese."

"Nonsenth! You can't talk to whaleth! There's no thuch thing as Whalethe!" shouted P'Klawz, who was so furious with Uncle Shawn that he couldn't help coming to the surface to yell more insults. "You're a fat, little badger!" But, as our pals watched, the great big eyes of Mr. Hubb got closer and closer to P'Klawz – and so did his great big mouth...

Mr. Hubb the whale swallowed Sylvester Pearlyclaws the Unusually Nasty man who pretended to be Dr. P'Klawz, even though that wasn't his name and he wasn't a doctor.

"I don't like thith!" said P'Klawz, his voice rather muffled because of being inside a whale. "I hate you all!"

The whale turned round in the water and flipped his great big tail goodbye and then swam away.

264

"I'll be back!"

"Goodness," said Bill. "That was Unusual."

"Maybe a little," said Uncle Shawn. "But then again, Mr. Hubb comes here a lot because I tell him jokes. All whales enjoy jokes."

"Do you think P'Klawz will be all right?"

"Oh, about as all right as he ever could be. Mr. Hubb will swim far away, and by the time he spits him out (I'm sure he tastes very bad and sour) P'Klawz might have learned to be nicer. Or he might at least have learned some jokes."

And for a while, Bill and Uncle Shawn watched Sam dancing with the bit of thin air that was actually Sky, her footsteps showing along the sand.

"I'm here!" Sky shouted, delighted.

"You're there!" shouted Sam.

And while Sky hugged her brother and Ginalolobrigida trotted over to see what the fuss was about, tossing her glossy fur in the breeze like a real film star, Sam made sure to sound a bit like a pirate being happy. "Woo-hoo! Avast! Shiver me timbers! Hooray, hooray, hooray!" 🐾

HAPPY BADGER DANCING

SECTION THIRTY-THREE

In which everyone on Uncle Shawn's llama farm, way up on the sunny side of Scotland, is so happy their toes feel ticklish. The sea is winking at the sun and the sky is as blue as blueberry jam in a big blue bucket. It really couldn't be a better end to the day for everyone.

Later, much later, everyone danced the Clog and Smock Dance to "This Badger's Gotta Move" – especially Bill, who was not a shy dancer anymore. Then everyone went home to bed. The llamas went back to the llama barns and Carlos was nice to Guinevere, and Guinevere was kind

267

to Carlos, and Ginalolobrigida Llama was just as fond of herself as she ever had been.

And when Brian got back to his barn, he found there was a message written in spider silk that said:

THE WORLD ASSOCIATION OF SPIDERS (PANDRUMDROOCHIT BRANCH) & YOUR PAL CLAUDE WILL ALWAYS WATCH OVER YOU SLEEP WELL

This was a little Unusual. But there's nothing wrong with being a little Unusual. And sometimes Brian would wake up at night and see friendly spider eyes winking at him, and he would

268

try to be brave about having a spider in his barn. "Because I am a brave llama who helped rescue Uncle Shawn. And so did the spiders."

And Mr. Hubb was already out at sea, sleeping on the ocean bed – and maybe P'Klawz was asleep, too.

And Sam and Sky were dreaming in spare beds in the farmhouse – which always had room for guests, especially Unusual guests. There was a dent where Sky's invisible head rested on her pillow.

After all their Unusual adventures, Uncle Shawn and Bill sat watching the sunset – Uncle Shawn in his big Uncle rocking chair and Bill in his little badger rocking chair.

"I'm so glad you're back," said Bill.

"And I'm so glad to be back. I missed you very much," said Uncle Shawn.

"And I missed you, too. We all did," said Bill, and he squeezed Uncle Shawn's hand.

"But now Pandrumdroochit and you and me and everyone can be however we want to be," said Uncle Shawn.

"Everyone can even be Unusual, if they like," said Bill.

"Which is just about usual for around here," said Uncle Shawn. "As long as we have a lot of happiness. That's the best of all."

And as the sun sank lower and lower and the fireflies started to shine and hum little songs, Bill asked, "What goes click, click, click, click, click, click, click, clack?"

"A spider with a wooden leg!" Uncle Shawn laughed. "And what else goes click, click, click, click, click, click, click, clack?"

"An octopus knitting socks and dropping a stitch!"

"Or eight mice biting toffee, only one of them got a soft caramel!" Uncle Shawn giggled. "Oh, it's good to have a best friend. A best friend you can tell jokes to and who will rescue you and sit with you and watch sunsets."

"Yes," said Badger Bill. "That's so true it's Pajimminy-Crimminy Unusually True."

And they rocked in their rocking chairs and listened to the llamas snoring in the llama barns and were very, very happy indeed.

In fact they were Pajimminy-Crimminy Unusually Happy. 🐾

A. L. KENNEDY

A. L. Kennedy was born in a small Scottish town far too long ago and has written books for adults and children, but mainly adults. Before that she made up stories to amuse herself. It has always surprised her that her job involves doing one of the things she loves most and she's very grateful to be a writer. She has won awards for her books in several countries. She has traveled all over the world and enjoyed it immensely. She plays the banjo badly, but makes up for this by never playing it anywhere near anyone else.

GEMMA CORRELL

Gemma Correll is a cartoonist, writer, illustrator and all-round small person. She is author of *A Pug's Guide to Etiquette* and *Doodling for Dog People*, and the illustrator of *Pig and Pug* by Lynne Berry, *Being a Girl* by Hayley Long and *The Trials of Ruby P. Baxter* (among other things). Her illustrations look like a five-year-old drew them because she hires one to do all her work for her. She pays him in fudge. His name is Alan.